SNOW GLOBE SECRETS

LAURA THOMAS

SNOW GLOBE SECRETS by LAURA THOMAS

ANAIAH SEASONAL

An imprint of ANAIAH PRESS, LLC.

7780 49th ST N. #129

Pinellas Park, FL 33781

This book is a work of fiction. All characters, places, names, and events are either a product of the author's imagination or are used fictitiously. Any likeness to any events, locations, or persons, alive or otherwise, is entirely coincidental.

Snow Globe Secrets copyright © 2023 Laura Thomas

All rights reserved, including the right to reproduce this book or portions thereof in any form. For inquiries and information, address Anaiah Press, LLC., 7780 49th ST N. #129 Pinellas Park, Florida, 33781

First Anaiah Seasonal edition November 2023

Edited by Kara Leigh Miller

Book Design by Anaiah Press

Cover Design by Anaiah Press

In memory of our own sweet English bulldog, Lily.
(2011-2023)

ACKNOWLEDGMENTS

There's something magical about writing a Christmas story, and I'm delighted to bring readers back to my home province of British Columbia, Canada, for another exciting novella! My humble thanks to:

Anaiah Press—my amazing publisher of this fifth book in the "Flight to Freedom" series. Thank you for your encouragement and confidence in me as an author—it means the world!

Kara Leigh Miller—my eagle-eyed editor who shook the snow globe just enough to make a perfect flurry of mystery and mistletoe!

Blossom Turner—who sees the very worst versions of my writing as my amazing critique partner... thank you, dear friend!

Charlotte, Jameson, and Jacob—for cheering on your mom and giving me the very best family Christmases... here's to many, many more!

Lyndon—my oh-so-patient husband of 35 years(!), for loving me well, for being my number one fanboy, for making every Christmas special, and for giving me my own Happily Ever After... I love you!

My Heavenly Father—for giving me light and life and words.

"God, investigate my life;
get all the facts firsthand.
I'm an open book to you;
even from a distance, you know what I'm thinking.
You know when I leave and when I get back;
I'm never out of your sight."
Psalm 139:1-3, The Message

CHAPTER ONE

Merry Christmas to me.

Alexis James smoothed the cherry-red ribbon on the Christmas gift—the one she always purchased for herself—and her heart thawed for the briefest of moments. She spun from the counter and marched through the bookstore, open cashmere coat flowing in her wake as her fingernails tapped a staccato beat on the precious paper package. Ignoring a gaggle of gossiping customers, Alexis lifted her chin, tugged the doorknob, and exited to the familiar jangle of silver bells overhead.

A whoosh of frigid air.

A crack of gunfire.

A squeal of tires.

Alexis dropped her gift and sank to the frozen ground. Her ears rang, and her pulse pounded.

God, help us.

For a heartbeat, the world seemed to stop spinning, and then muffled shouts split the silence.

"Alexis?" Her sister's strangled voice drifted out from the bookstore.

"Carla?" The weight of her sister's hand lay heavy on Alexis's shoulder. "I'm okay." Alexis took a few seconds to orient herself and covered Carla's hand with her own. She *was* all right, wasn't she?

Letting out a slow, shuddering breath, Alexis straightened on unsteady legs and shook her coat sleeve free of glass shards from the broken storefront window. She checked the street to the left. The vehicle was long gone.

"Thank goodness. When I heard the shot—" Carla enveloped Alexis in a tight hug. The sobs of a child sounded from the store. "I need to check on the customers. Come with me?"

Alexis stood glued to the spot, uncharacteristically unsure of what to do. "Go ahead. Give me a minute."

"Don't be long. You'll catch cold out here." Carla rushed back inside.

Someone wailed. Alexis shivered. Was this how people felt in war times when bombs dropped? Maybe she'd read one too many WWII novels of late. She shook the fuzziness from her mind and turned her attention to the glass-littered sidewalk to her right, in front of the Happily Ever After bookstore.

A man's limp form lay face down on the snow, and a gasp escaped Alexis's lips. *"No."* Her wrapped package had landed next to him. She spotted a young couple across the street who stood gawking at the spectacle. "Call 9-1-1. *Now.*"

The police station was two minutes away, but someone had to take charge. Alexis yelled through the smashed window. "Everyone stay where you are. Don't panic."

She stepped over to the prone body and crouched down next to him. No movement. And now, the white snow beneath him was stained red in an oval-shaped patch by his head. *Please let him be alive.* The red ribbon unfurled from her package and mingled with the blood. All the red and the white... this was not good. "Sir?"

Nothing.

Only the garbled voices of bystanders and customers and—where was the ambulance?

She pressed trembling fingers onto the side of his neck and closed her eyes. Yes. A rhythm. Surely, if the window smashed, the bullet—and only one shot was lodged in her memory— must have merely grazed the man. Unless the bullet went straight through him...

Alexis knew better than to try to move an injured body, so she placed a hand on his broad back to let him know he wasn't alone. She would want someone to reassure her of that.

"You're not alone. I'm right here. You're not alone." Her fingers tingled. His coat was high-end. She knew the feel of a decent cashmere wool blend, and this man, she guessed to be in his mid-thirties, had taste.

"Alexis? What are you doing?"

Her head snapped up at the sound of David's voice. Officer Baxter; he was in uniform.

He stomped over stray slivers of glass with heavy boots and offered his hand. "You okay? Are you hurt?"

"Where's the ambulance? This guy is in bad shape." Alexis detested the tremor in her voice. "I'm fine, but he's obviously not."

"I've got this." A young woman with blonde, frizzy hair ushered Alexis from the cold ground and toward David. "I'm a paramedic. Off duty, but I'll take over until the ambulance arrives."

"Thanks," David spoke for them both.

Alexis glanced back into the store, where Carla and two

other police officers attempted to rally the shaken cluster of customers. Who could have imagined the possibility of a shooting in Hollybrook a week before Christmas?

"Alexis?" David took her by the shoulders and lowered his voice. "Do you need to get checked out at the hospital?" He picked a piece of glass from her long hair.

"I told you, I'm fine. It was a shock, that's all." She shrugged free from his hands. "I don't remember when something like this last happened in our town. A shooting?" She collected her leather purse from the ground and gave it a good shake. "I don't think the man is a local. What do you think—drug-related?" Drug money might explain the coat...

"That's exactly what we'll investigate." David tugged a little notebook from his jacket pocket and slid a pen from its spine. "Can you tell me what you saw? The 9-1-1 caller said there was a gunshot, and someone drove off in a hurry. Did you get a look at the vehicle or anything at all?"

Alexis squeezed her eyes shut for a moment. "Red? Maybe a flash of red as I heard the tires peel away? I can't be certain. It's pretty dark out here already, even with the streetlamps on." She bit her lower lip. "I'm really not sure. It happened so fast. And then there was the red on the snow... the ribbon, the blood..." Her knees buckled.

David caught her before she collapsed.

Alexis's chin trembled. "I don't know what's the matter with me."

"Hey, witnessing a shooting is a big deal. Probably a good idea to speak to someone about it."

Alexis James did *not* need help. And she did not need David the Protector. She regained her balance, even in her high-heeled leather boots, and pulled away from his strong arms. "I told you I don't need a doctor."

He raised his brows so they disappeared beneath the peak of his RCMP hat.

"Oh, you mean a therapist?" Alexis placed a hand on one hip. "I think not."

"Or maybe talk with your little sister?" David nodded at Carla as she hurried toward them, worry etched in her chocolate-brown eyes.

"How's that poor man?" Carla's face paled as the ambulance pulled up. "Do we know who he is?"

Alexis peered around David's six-foot-four frame. "Hard to tell until they put him on the stretcher, but I don't recognize him." She shivered as the stranger was moved with caution, neck brace in place. That was something—at least he really was breathing, and it wasn't her imagination. Alexis was a realtor, not a doctor. "There. I think he moved his arm. He must be coming around. He was definitely out cold."

"Let's move on, folks. Nothing to see here." David pushed back the curious crowd now forming along the sidewalk. "You'd think Christmas shoppers would be anxious to get on with their business."

"In this town?" Alexis gritted her teeth. "Are you kidding? They live for all the gossip they can get." And she would know.

David ambled off with his notebook, and Carla reached for Alexis's hand. She gave it a squeeze. "You're freezing. Why don't you come on inside the store? We may be missing a window, but it's still warmer than standing out here." She bent down and retrieved Alexis's dropped package. "Oh, sis, your snow globe." She shook the box, and the rattle confirmed the broken contents. "It's shattered. I'm so sorry. I know this was super expensive."

Alexis drew back her shoulders. "No big deal." The

snow globe *was* a big deal. No one understood why. "I'll come inside in a minute. You go ahead." She enveloped her sweet sister in another hug. Life was as fragile as her snow globe. "Love you."

"Love you, too." Carla kissed her cheek. "Don't be long. I have to make some calls and get this window fixed. Old Mr. Wiebe is going to be heartbroken knowing his beloved bookstore was a crime scene."

"Coming through." The paramedics wheeled the stretcher toward the waiting ambulance, and Alexis craned her neck to check on the victim. She couldn't make out his entire face as it was partially covered by the neck brace, but he was handsome. No doubt about that. She blinked. He looked familiar somehow.

Who was this intriguing man—and why on earth did someone in Hollybrook want him dead?

CHAPTER TWO

After a fitful night of tossing and turning amidst several variations of being shot in her vivid dreams, Alexis threw back the duvet and changed into her workout gear. Not that she was feeling particularly energetic, but she would push through. Like always. She followed the rich aroma of freshly brewed coffee and the soft strains of Christmas carols as she padded down the spiral staircase and rounded the corner into her spacious kitchen.

"Morning." Carla beamed.

After living alone for so long, Alexis was getting used to being greeted each new day by her little sister. "Hey."

"Let me make you a coffee." Carla set down her own gray snowflake-covered mug on the kitchen island and bustled over to the chic coffee station. "You know I love being your personal barista."

Attempting to argue was a useless endeavor. Alexis had tried. "Thanks. You're the best. A skinny cappuccino would be great." She sank onto a stool and tied her hair in a high ponytail with a band from her wrist. "You know I'm going to miss this when you're a married woman and have a husband to fuss over."

Carla pulled her turquoise glasses from her face and cleaned the lenses on a tea towel while the machine ground the beans. "Eight more sleeps, and I get to be Mrs. Rhys Templeton. Finally." Her cheeks pinked, an adorable look on her. "But I'm more concerned about you, Lex. After being that close to a shooting yesterday?" She slid on her glasses and pulled another snowflake mug from an open shelf. "Did you manage to sleep at all last night?"

A shudder ran up Alexis's spine. The whole thing was harrowing. A shooting outside the Happily Ever After bookstore in sleepy Hollybrook. Seriously? But she wasn't about to add to her sister's anxiety a week before the wedding. "I'm all right. Let's hope the incident was a random drug deal gone bad with some out-of-towner."

"I guess. I'm thankful no one else got injured. Can you believe they found the bullet lodged in a copy of *The Christmas Carol* of all things?"

"Appropriate for the season, I suppose."

Carla completed the drink with an impressive swirl of foam and slid the mug in front of Alexis. "But imagine if old Mr. Wiebe had positioned one of his special rare books at the front of the store? They're super valuable. I know he keeps most of them up in his safe, but he often brings one down to have on display. Says book lovers need to be able to enjoy *all* the books."

Alexis knew Mr. Wiebe owned an extensive collection in his apartment above the store. The unassuming elderly man had to be worth a small fortune.

Carla pulled a couple of yogurts from the fridge. "Parfait?"

"I'll wait until later, thanks."

Alexis had a huge surprise to share with her sister. She'd planned on waiting until after the wedding... but maybe they needed a little joy after yesterday's sinister incident.

Alexis went to pick up the mug. Her fingers trembled. She ran her hands down her leggings instead. "That man is lucky he has you."

"Rhys?"

"No, well, yes. But I mean old Mr. Wiebe. You've done wonders for the bookstore in the past six months." She cupped the mug again and willed her fingers to calm down.

"Thanks. The job's been so perfect for me. Covering a maternity leave that happened to coincide with the exact time I was staying in town with you? I used to dream about working in the bookstore when we were kids."

"You always were kinda weird."

Carla wrinkled her nose. "You always were kinda mean." She dumped blueberries on top of her granola mixture and joined Alexis at the island. "And by the way, you can't hide the fact your hands are quivering, and you're as pale as the milk I frothed for your coffee."

Darn it. So much for being the protective big sis. "I'll feel better after a workout."

Carla raised a brow. "Can't you give yourself a little grace the morning after you witnessed a *shooting*? I would be comforting myself with a warm, gooey cinnamon bun about now."

"We can't all have a dream metabolism like yours, you know. I have to stay on top of my exercise regime." She sat a little taller on the stool. "Besides, you were there yesterday, too."

"At the back of the store. And I didn't get a close-up of the victim. Speaking of whom, I wonder how that man is doing." Carla squinted. "And who he is. Such a mystery."

"I intend to find out." Alexis lifted her mug with both hands, now desperate for a shot of caffeine. The first taste ran down her throat, warm and soothing. "I'm going to the hospital this morning."

"You are? How come?"

Another sip. "I think I recognized him from somewhere, but I need to be sure. Plus, if he is a stranger in town, he won't have any other visitors now, will he?" She set down the mug and inspected her perfect red fingernails.

Carla placed a hand on her sister's arm. "No offense, but I don't think you'll fool anyone at the hospital if you say you're there purely as a concerned citizen."

Alexis sniffed. "You're right. Visiting the sick is not my thing. But I may be able to help if he needs to find a place to rent in case he has to recuperate or something."

"Ever the businesswoman." Carla chuckled.

"Always. I worked a good deal for you and Rhys with the cabin, did I not?" Alexis shifted on her stool. "And while we're on the subject of business deals, I have news."

"Another success story in the real estate world?"

Alexis focused on her coffee mug and took a deep breath. Sharing was new. Even with her sister. Alexis had been fiercely independent and untouchable for so long, but this was her attempt at doing something meaningful. Something that might make a difference in her community. Maybe even be accepted...

"Umm, you're killing me here with the dramatic pause." Carla held her spoon mid-air.

"Sorry." Alexis raised her chin and grinned. "I bought the bookstore."

Carla's mouth fell open, and she dropped her spoon on the countertop. "You what?" She jumped off her stool, squealed in a pitch only detectable by canines, and smothered Alexis with a hug. "For real? You purchased Happily Ever After from Mr. Wiebe?"

"I did. Well, the deal's in process, and I officially take ownership on the first of January." Alexis's insides warmed. She knew she'd made the right decision, and her sister's reaction was confirmation.

"I can't believe he finally sold to someone. Hasn't the business been in the Wiebe family for generations?" Carla settled back in her seat. "So, is this an investment, or are you going to be hands-on?"

"Believe it or not, I've been dreaming about this for a while. I have some cool ideas for the store, and for the community, too. I've been slowing down my real estate business and plan on spending most of my time at the store. But don't worry, I'm going to treat the bookstore's legacy with the respect it deserves."

"I know you will. And I'm so proud of you."

Alexis crossed her legs. "Thanks. Mr. Wiebe is one of the few humans in this town who treats me with kindness. He knows as well as anyone else what I was like in my youth—but he accepts me for who I am today. We have this… connection."

He loved her fascination with snow globes and always went above and beyond to help her procure whatever she selected from around the world.

"Mr. Wiebe is one in a million, for sure." Carla chewed on a thumbnail. "But I'm sorry you still feel unaccepted here after all this time. People can be cruel."

"Tell me about it." Although, maybe her plans for the bookstore would change everything. "Anyway, please inform Mr. Wiebe that if there's anything I can do with the window repairs, he need only ask. I have contacts. And the week before Christmas is not a good time for a storefront to look like it's part of a mafia scene."

"I will. That's kind of you."

Alexis winked. "Ever the businesswoman."

"Wow. You bought a bookstore. I'm in shock. Does Jennifer or any of the part-timers know?"

"Jennifer might. Or she may at least have her suspicions—there's something funky going on with her lately. She gives me the deep freeze whenever I come in for meetings with Mr. Wiebe. I suppose he could have already shared the news with her."

"Or she may have figured it out for herself. She's worked there for years, and not much gets past that girl." Carla spooned the last of her breakfast in her mouth and deposited her dishes in the sink. "I wouldn't worry about Jennifer. Apparently, she's got some new love in her life and seems distracted most of the time."

"Maybe that's it."

"Well, I have to head over to the bookstore for an hour this morning to make sure everything's in order before I finish there for good." Carla pivoted toward Alexis. "Although when you're the boss, perhaps you can call on me once in a while. I think I might enjoy an occasional shift."

"You think we could work together?"

Carla grimaced. "I'm getting flashbacks from our lemonade stand joint venture when we were kids. Let me think about that... But I'd like to come with you to the hospital today."

"Do you think I need babysitting?" Alexis hopped down from the stool and stretched her aching arms above her head.

"No." Carla bit her bottom lip. "I think you're a lot

more shaken up by the shooting than you'll ever let on, though. And after everything you've done for me as chief wedding planner these past months, the least I can do is tag along while you put your mind at rest as to who the mystery man is. You need to be careful."

Alexis scowled. "I'm not some crazed man-hunter. You know that, right? When was the last time I even went on a date?" Surely, her own sister wasn't still holding her colorful past against her.

"I know, I'm sorry. You're right. I don't want to see you get hurt again. That's all. Let me come with you and see who this tall, dark, handsome stranger is?"

"Fine." Alexis plodded toward the stairs leading down to her home gym and then spun around. "Wait. Who says he's tall, dark, and handsome?"

Carla tugged her glasses to the end of her nose and peered over them. "Let's just say you have a type."

Tom Harrington's head pounded. This was not his bed. He felt along the edges with his fingers—the frame was tiny. Not a king-size or even a queen. The stale air smelled pungent yet familiar. If only he could muster the energy to open his eyes...

He was in a hospital? What the Dickens? He blinked several times and was rewarded by the obnoxious glare of fluorescent lights and a general hum of movement and muffled voices out in a corridor. The writer in him wanted to make a note of every sense that was now on high alert for the purpose of future reference. But how injured was he? Was he dying? He should call a nurse.

Tom went to reach toward a side table and winced. The

outside of his upper left arm smarted, and his eyes watered. He used his right hand to gingerly inspect the area with a run of his fingers over one section of the bandage. He almost jumped from the bed. Man, that was sore.

A gunshot. He'd been shot? That's right. Was this the Wild West? He studied the square ceiling tiles and thought back over yesterday. He was in Canada. Hollybrook. He'd arrived at the airport, figured out the car rental, and dumped his things at a quaint little hotel downtown.

Calling this place a city seemed a little generous, but a stroll around the town center proved Hollybrook to be utterly charming. Yes, he had walked at leisure in the snow —relishing the prospect of his first-ever white Christmas. The people seemed friendly enough, and he congratulated himself on finding the Happily Ever After bookstore. He had no intention of going inside. Not yet. He had to get his bearings first. Speak with a few locals. This was a matter of business but also a matter of the heart. Of history and family. He had to tread with the greatest of care.

But then the gunshot. One. Not serious enough to kill him. But somebody knew he was in Hollybrook. Knew his business. And apparently, the threats he received back in England were not idle and had now followed him across the ocean.

CHAPTER THREE

Alexis flipped down her truck's rearview mirror and checked her reflection. Immaculate. She'd made a little extra effort applying her makeup after showering post-exercise today. Not that she cared what this potentially tall, dark, handsome victim thought about her—he could be married, an axe murderer, or the usual self-centered jerk that she seemed to attract like honey to a grizzly bear. Also, he could have been badly injured, and she was anything but the nursing-back-to-health type.

"You don't have to come to the ward, you know." She glanced over at Carla, who tugged on a pair of black leather gloves. "You could grab a coffee at the cafeteria and read a book."

Carla guffawed. "As tempting as that sounds, I've tried the coffee here. It's nothing to rave about."

"You know, for someone who is generally content with the simple things in life, you're quite the coffee snob." Alexis opened the truck door and jumped down onto the packed snow. The icy wind almost took her breath away.

"It was the stint I did as a barrister while I was at

University," Carla shouted above the wind as she rubbed her gloved hands together. "Spoiled me for life."

They both tucked their chins beneath their scarves and scurried across the parking lot toward the hospital entrance.

"I'm not complaining. You make a fabulous cappuccino." Alexis shivered. "Let's get inside before we freeze."

The doors swooshed open, and Alexis led the way straight over to the stairwell. The wall of warmth was welcome, but the antiseptic smell of sickness curdled her stomach. Was this guy worth the effort? Frustrating as this whole thing was, she couldn't get that glimpse of his face out of her mind.

"Slow down, sis." Carla let out an exasperated burst of air. "I don't know how you get around so quickly in those heels. Not to mention in the snow."

Alexis admired her cognac leather ankle boots with their four-inch stacked heels. They were gorgeous. "I'm not hiking; I'm visiting. And I have a meeting in the office this afternoon. I like to make an effort."

"Unlike me?" Carla chuckled, but Alexis caught the hint of insecurity in her eyes. Her beautiful-inside-and-out sister should feel confident, particularly the week of her wedding.

"No. That's not what I meant at all." She linked an arm through Carla's and slowed her steps. Why did she always manage to say the wrong thing? Carla was the last person on the planet she wanted to hurt. "You don't even need to make an effort. Your beauty is natural. I would kill to have your flawless skin and naturally wavy hair like mom's. And *not* to have to work out like a maniac every single morning to stay in shape? Sign me up."

"Okay, okay." Carla patted Alexis's hand. "Enough with the back-peddling. It's all good. And for the record, I would break my neck if I tried stomping around in your footwear. I'll stick with my practical Chelsea boots."

"At least they're burgundy patent. You have fabulous style. Don't sell yourself short."

"Thanks. You've rubbed off on me a little the past few months." Carla stopped at the elevator, but Alexis pulled her past the huddle of people waiting.

"Nope. You know how I feel about elevators."

"Still?" Carla's eyes widened.

"Claustrophobia. It's a thing. Not as bad as it used to be, but I avoid elevators like the plague." She held open the door to the stairwell. "One of the pluses in moving back here after Vancouver. We don't have many high rises to contend with compared to major cities. Come on, the exercise will do you good."

"Thought I didn't need exercise."

Alexis groaned. "It's only two floors up."

"How do you know where this guy even is?"

Their footsteps echoed as they marched up the stairs in time with one another.

Alexis checked her phone. Nothing urgent. David Baxter could wait. "I called earlier and spoke to Jennifer's sister, Jane. She's on nurse duty on the second-floor desk and says our gunshot victim is there."

"How on earth did you manage to find that out?"

"I know pretty much everyone who's anyone in Hollybrook. It has its benefits." *And its perils.* Alexis held the door open for Carla.

"At least it's nice and toasty in here." Carla untied her burgundy plaid scarf as she walked onto the second floor.

"Toasty and stuffy. I hate hospitals."

"This guy must have made quite the impression, even

unconscious," Carla mumbled the words and received a jab from Alexis's elbow.

"Alexis? Hi." The perky young nurse wearing navy scrubs stopped in her tracks and shuffled a file of papers in the crook of her arm. "Thought I might bump into you this morning."

"Hi, Jane." Alexis offered her friendliest smile. "How is the new apartment? All settled in?"

"I adore it. I still can't believe I get to wake up to that view every morning. Thanks again."

Alexis shrugged. "I love matching people with their perfect homes. It's what I do." *For now, at least.* "Do you know my sister, Carla?"

Carla gave a tiny wave.

"I don't think we've met, but my sister, Jennifer, works at the bookstore and told me about you. You're the one getting married on Christmas Eve?" Jane's face lit up. "So romantic."

Alexis kept her impatient sighing to a minimum while she waited for them to finish gushing. "So... about the gunshot victim?"

Nurse Jane straightened. "Yes. Of course. Such a relief Jennifer was on a break when it happened." She looked at them both. "You two are okay? She told me all about it."

"We're fine. Thanks for asking. But I'm anxious to see the guy who was shot..."

"Sure." Jane walked down the corridor, and the sisters followed. "You ran it by Officer Baxter, right?"

Alexis cleared her throat. "I did."

Carla mouthed, "You did?"

"Sort of." Alexis texted David before she left home and mentioned she would swing by the hospital today. She hadn't been explicit with the details, but he would presume she was getting herself checked out. If this man was dangerous, police would be present anyway, and as far as she could see, today was just another regular Friday morning at Hollybrook Hospital.

"What do we know about him?" Carla asked. "Is he from around here?"

"Definitely not." Jane's face flushed. "He's rather dreamy, actually. And he hasn't had any visitors, other than the police, of course. I'm sure he'll be happy to have you ladies checking in on him."

Interesting. The authorities must be satisfied after questioning him. Alexis bit her lower lip. "Hey, Carla, would you mind if I go in to see him first? In case he's not feeling great or it's overwhelming or—"

"You want me to get you a very average cup of hospital coffee?" Carla smirked.

"That would be lovely. Thank you."

Jane nodded past the nurses' station, bedazzled with silver tinsel. "There's a vending machine at the end of this corridor."

"I'll take my time." Carla gave Alexis a wink before strolling away.

"And here we are. He's the only occupant." Jane knocked on the open door to a small private room. "Visitor for you." She turned to Alexis. "I'll be at the nurses' station if you need me."

Alexis took a deep breath and breezed into the small mushroom-colored room. A solitary bed flanked with pale blue curtains occupied the space, and to her surprise, the man sat upright and wide awake.

"Oh, h-hello." What had she expected? Not this. Not a fine specimen with his groomed short beard and trendy haircut, appearing healthy and handsome, even in a blue hospital gown.

"Good morning. Can I help you?"

My word. He has an English accent, too. "No, well, actually, it was I who was hoping to help you, but it looks as if you're feeling much better than yesterday." A patch of gauze was taped to one side of his forehead, but other than that, he seemed unscathed. And still familiar in a way she couldn't quite put her finger on.

"Yesterday? Were you there? When I was... shot? Wait, do I know you?" He moved forward and then winced and settled back against his pillow.

"Headache?" Alexis leaned against the end of the bed.

"Bit of a concussion, apparently. Not too bad, though."

"Nasty. At least it wasn't a bullet." She attempted a smile.

"The bullet just left a graze." The man lifted the loose sleeve of his left arm and revealed a white bandage, as well as a well-toned muscular arm. "But I'm grateful. It could have been so much worse. My granny must have been praying for me."

Adorable. "I'm Alexis, by the way. Alexis James. And I was the one who found you on the ground outside the bookstore. You scared the living daylights out of me. I thought from all the blood..."

"So you saw everything? The getaway car or whoever had the gun?" His face turned whiter than the silk blouse she was wearing. "Did they see you?"

"I don't think so. It's all a blur, to be honest. I was leaving the bookstore, heard the shot, ducked, dropped my snow globe, which smashed—"

"Sorry about that. I love snow globes. So nostalgic."

"Right?" A hunky man who appreciated snow globes.

How attractive. "Anyway, the next second, I heard someone drive away in a hurry. Then I saw you."

He ran a hand down his face. "And you're okay?"

"I'm perfectly fine. Really, I am."

"Well, first of all, thank you. And you must let me replace your snow globe."

"Absolutely not." He would have a conniption if he knew how much she spent on her snow globes. "I don't want anything. I was checking to see how you were, that's all."

"What an angel you are." He rewarded her with a grin.

Yes, he checked off the dark and handsome boxes. And from her estimation, the tall was a given, too. "Thanks. Literally no one has called me an angel before. Ever."

"It wasn't as bad as it must have appeared. They tell me I face-planted onto the snow—presumably, I slipped when the bullet nicked my arm—and must have knocked myself out on a rock or something. There's a bit of a gash on my forehead that took some stitches, but truly, other than a headache and a sore arm, I'm feeling ready to leave this place."

"Not a fan of hospitals?"

He lowered his gaze but not before Alexis caught a hint of deep sadness. "No. Not a fan." He focused on the thin, blue blanket covering his legs.

A silent moment followed, and Alexis had a sudden urge to give him a hug. Ridiculous. She slid the cream wool scarf from her neck and folded it over her arm. Goodness, this room was warm. "So, are you new in town? Visiting for Christmas?"

He looked up. "Where are my manners? Please, take a seat." He motioned to the hard, plastic chair at his side.

"I don't want to intrude." She batted her lashes out of habit.

"No, really. I'm waiting to be discharged. No point in taking up a hospital bed."

"In that case..." She placed her leather purse on the floor and set her scarf on top.

"You can tell I'm not a local then?" A smile twitched on his lips.

"Honestly, it's not only your accent. I know many families in Hollybrook after being born and raised here, and I tend to get to know the newbies in town. Part of the job."

"Which is?" He tilted his head in a most appealing manner.

"Realtor. I make it my business to know what's going on in this little city, and quite frankly, we don't often have shootings outside the Happily Ever After bookstore." She matched his head tilt with one of her own.

"Fair comment." He shifted to face her better and then grimaced at the change in position.

"Can I pass you some water? See if the nurse can get you some pain meds or anything?" Alexis surprised herself at this caring side she didn't know she possessed. But he was enchanting and emanated all the vulnerable vibes in his little blue gown.

His piercing green eyes twinkled. "That's kind, but I think I'll wait as long as I can for more meds. And to answer your question, yes, I am visiting. From the UK."

Alexis settled back into her chair. "I got the UK bit. Do you have family here?"

He squinted. "It's complicated. But I'm here to do some... research of sorts. A working vacation. And as I'm sure you're dying to know about the shooting but are way too sweet to ask..."

Alexis shifted in her chair. Sure, she was *way* too sweet.

"I truly don't know who the individual was with the gun. I only flew in yesterday, and as I explained to the police, I'm not involved with anything drug-related or dangerous. I leave that to my imagination."

"What do you mean?" Alexis crossed one skinny jean-clad leg over the other. "Your imagination?"

He lifted a shoulder. "I'm a writer."

Was that why she thought she recognized him? Her jaw dropped, but she made a quick recovery. "Wait, what's your name?" How had she not even asked that yet?

"Tom Harrington."

No way. "That's why you looked familiar. I've seen your face on a bunch of book covers. Good grief, how did I not put two and two together? I'm a huge fan. Huge. And I've read all of your books. WWII fiction is my favorite genre to read. Your last one..." She tapped her chin. "Don't tell me, don't tell me... *The Paris* something-or-other. I devoured it. *The Paris Whisperer.*" She jumped up from her chair. "Yes, *The Paris Whisperer.* It was a crazy bestseller."

Tom let out a chuckle. "That's the one."

Alexis checked herself. Since when did she get this excited about anyone or anything? Good grief. "Sorry about that." She lowered herself back down and smoothed her black cashmere coat on either side of her. "Tom Harrington. It's a pleasure to meet you, and I'm very glad you dodged a bullet yesterday. Literally."

"Thanks."

Was he blushing? This world-famous author who must have a constant stream of admirers in his daily life.

"So, where are you staying? Are you on a book tour or something?" Alexis tried to temper down her inner fangirl, but keeping her cool was a challenge.

"No. This isn't work. Actually, I hoped to keep my presence low-key. Thankfully, the average non-WWII-fiction-lover wouldn't know me from Adam. I spoke with the police, and they're trying to keep this incident out of the press as much as possible."

Alexis almost choked. "It's not the press you have to worry about; this city's rumor mill is a well-oiled machine, and word-of-mouth is a rushing river running through it." She swallowed her frustration. "But I'll do what I can to help freeze the flow. They don't call me ice queen for nothing." She lifted her chin.

Tom narrowed his eyes. "Ice queen? Interesting. And I appreciate that. I'd love to have a few days of peace, at least. I'm staying at a charming little hotel in town for the next night, and then I've rented a place in the mountains. Hoping to get some writing done there."

Alexis played with a strand of long hair. "Do you mind if I ask where exactly, if it's not too stalker-ish? I'd hate for you to have a less-than-stellar experience while you're in Hollybrook."

"I forget the address, but it's on some lake..." He wrinkled his nose. "Clearwater Crescent? The internet insists it's picture-perfect and only about a half-hour drive from town."

Alexis gasped. "That's my rental. Not my property; I mean, it's one I rent out for the owner. You're going to love it. And I'm presuming you used an alias for the booking. Of course, you did."

He nodded. "It's usually safer that way, not to bring attention to myself and fly under the radar, so to speak."

She caught a fleeting presence of fear in those green eyes. Had he experienced problems in the past being a famous author? Poor guy.

"And the name I use is thoroughly void of imagination."

Alexis recalled her to-do list for tomorrow. "Don't tell me... you're John Smith?"

He grimaced. "Guilty."

"Mr. Harrington?" A white-haired doctor entered the room and peered over the top of his gold-rimmed glasses. "Mind if I give one final check before we send you on your way?"

"I should leave you to it." Alexis gathered her things and dug into her purse. "Here's my business card, Tom. Please call if you need help or don't get the go-ahead to drive yet. I believe I have *Mr. Smith* down for tomorrow afternoon to get settled into the rental. Does that work?"

"Thanks very much, yes. It was lovely to meet you. I'll call you tomorrow." He touched her sleeve as she stood, and his eyes bore into hers. "Please, be very careful, won't you?"

Alexis froze, her mouth bone-dry. "Sure. You, too."

She turned and nodded at the doctor on her way out of the room. Once in the hallway, she stopped and stared at the tiled floor for a moment. If he had no clue who shot him yesterday, what was that last look he gave her? Was it friendly concern—or legitimate fear?

CHAPTER FOUR

"Are you done already?"

Alexis looked up as Carla walked toward her, clutching two lidded drinks.

"Yes, and wait 'til you hear what I found out." Alexis accepted one cup of something that smelled more like cocoa than coffee. "Hot chocolate?"

Carla took a sip of hers. "I have it on good authority that it's a safer option than the questionable coffee. Are we heading home?"

"Smells good. And yes, I'll drop you home, and then I need to get to a work meeting." Alexis picked up the pace and nodded at Jane, who was on the phone at the nurses' station. "And then I'm having an early night. All this excitement is making my head ache."

"So, spill the details. Who's the mystery man? Are you going to be his Florence Nightingale?" Carla reached the stairwell first and held the door open.

Alexis stopped for effect and surveyed the hallway to make sure no one was in earshot. "He's Tom Harrington."

Carla's jaw dropped. "Like, the author?"

"The very same." Alexis tossed back her hair and sashayed through the doorway. "And I gave him my business card."

Alexis started down the stairs, careful not to upset her drink. She didn't trust these lids. Carla was a bigger bookworm than she was. No surprise Carla knew exactly who Alexis was talking about.

"Wow. That's crazy. Why would Tom Harrington be in Hollybrook?"

Alexis took her time descending the stairs in high heels. "Why not? I happen to know for a fact we have a number of celebrities who own some of the mega-million-dollar lakeside properties, even if they only spend a few weeks in them each year. How do you think I managed to do so well here in real estate?"

Carla grabbed Alexis's arm. "Hold on. His latest book. The one that was really popular."

"The Paris Whisperer?"

"That's the one. Lex, I always said you are a dead ringer for the woman on the cover. Long blonde hair, red lipstick and all. Remember?"

"I guess." She would be checking out that little nugget, for sure. Did Tom Harrington see the resemblance?

"Does he have a place here? Why would someone shoot him? What did he tell you?"

Alexis took great delight in sharing all the details with her sister on their drive back to the house, knowing full well Carla was the most trustworthy person in the world and would never talk of it with anyone else. Other than her fiancé, maybe. Carla was such a good Christian girl and everything lovely that was lacking in Alexis. How could two sisters be so different?

That evening, Alexis relished some alone time after a flurry of meetings, phone calls, and paperwork. *I'm more than ready for a new chapter in my work life.* She grinned at her bookish pun. One more open house tomorrow morning, and she would wind things down for the holidays.

She puttered around her lavish bedroom, closing blinds and turning on lamps. A cozy night at home sounded perfect. Planning Carla and Rhys's wedding on top of a heavy workload was taking its toll on her. Who had time to think about Christmas? Now, even her new snow globe was smashed. She let out a heavy breath at the disappointment of not being able to add that little beauty to her collection. *I'll order a replacement tonight.*

Alexis changed into her black silk pajamas and headed downstairs. She paused at the recess in the kitchen, where a spectacular shelving unit displayed her snow globe collection from around the world. These domes of delight were the only things she was sentimental about. Yesterday's broken purchase tugged at her heartstrings. She gave her head a shake and grabbed some food from the kitchen counter on her way to the great room.

A glass of white wine in hand and a charcuterie board for one, she sank down onto her cream leather sofa and sighed with contentment. Lily, her English bulldog, plodded over from her favorite spot in front of the roaring fireplace and clambered up next to Alexis with no small amount of effort and guttural groaning.

"Hey, Lily. I bet your day was more leisurely than mine." Alexis set her snacks on the glass coffee table and tickled her dog's velvety ears. "Missed me? Don't worry, we're going to have a chill girls' night. The two of us."

Alexis picked up her glass and took a long sip of a delicious local chardonnay, one of the perks of living in wine country where vineyards were plentiful. She inhaled the soothing scent wafting over from her vanilla spice candle and closed her eyes.

The moment of bliss was short-lived as her phone blared an upbeat Christmas tune—Carla's idea of a festive joke—and she checked the caller ID. David. Again. Really? He'd tried her multiple times this afternoon already. *Let's get this over with.*

"David. Hi." She tried to sound enthusiastic, but her tone was unconvincing even to her own ears.

"Alexis? Finally, I've been trying to get hold of you all day."

"Sorry. I was working." She took another sip for fortification. "What's up?"

"Seriously? I got your cryptic text this morning and then found out from Jane at the hospital that you'd been in to see the gunshot victim. And I presume you had no intention of getting yourself checked out." He let out a sharp huff. "Why do you refuse to play by the rules?"

Alexis set her wine glass on the coffee table and picked up a cracker topped with aged cheddar and a blob of red pepper jelly. Her stomach rumbled. "I was being a concerned citizen. I saw the man being shot yesterday, for goodness' sake."

"And kindness comes so naturally to you?"

Wow. That stung. She bit into the cracker and allowed him time to regret his little quip.

"I'm sorry. I didn't mean it that way. I'm looking out for you, that's all."

Alexis swallowed her food. "I've told you a hundred

times that I do *not* need a protector. Besides, it was a random shooting. Wrong time, wrong place."

An exaggerated exhale sounded over the phone. "Seems a coincidence; a stranger in town and some drive-by shooting. I'm guessing you're familiar with his books, this Harrington guy. You always liked that war fiction."

"Yes, I'm familiar. He's a bestselling author. Brilliant. And he's asked to keep his identity quiet as much as possible. You probably know that. He's a nice guy. Give him a break. He's supposed to be on vacation, and it's Christmas."

"Tell that to Mr. Wiebe, as he has to reassure his customers of their safety and then get his bookstore window fixed in his busiest week of the year."

Alexis licked her fingers. She knew the window was being repaired tomorrow, and earlier today, she'd reassured Mr. Wiebe that the hoopla wouldn't keep the shoppers away. And if it did, well, she would make sure January was the best month the bookstore had ever experienced.

"Don't worry. It'll draw a crowd. You know how the locals love a bit of drama." She'd been the cause of many a drama in past years, and David knew it. "The juicier, the better. Lots of loose lips..."

"Alexis." His raised voice caused Lily to growl. The dog despised David Baxter. "Is that hound of yours baring her teeth at the mere sound of my voice?"

Alexis kissed the top of Lily's head. "What can I say? The dog has taste. Listen, thanks for checking in, but I have things to do. Have a great evening."

Without waiting for a response, Alexis cut him off and dropped her phone on the sofa, the other side of Lily. "Come on, girl, it's time for a sappy Christmas movie, a big bar of chocolate, and a snuggle. Promise you won't tell anyone I've gone soft, okay?"

❄

Saturday morning dawned merry and bright as the sun reflected off a fresh layer of snow. Alexis squinted at the glare through her bedroom window as she watched Carla drive away to meet Rhys. The besotted couple were going for a final snowshoe session before they became man and wife next Saturday. This week would be a whirlwind of last-minute details to arrange, problem-solving, loved ones flying in, her bachelorette night, and whatever else they could squeeze into seven days.

Thank goodness this was the last morning Alexis would have to focus on her job. Not that sitting in an empty house required too much focus. December was a slow time of year—who wanted to view a house when Christmas shopping, baking, caroling, and wrapping needed to be done?

Alexis giggled at herself as she applied her favorite red lipstick. What did she know about such festivities? Yes, the Christmas tree was up, and her home looked like something in the glossy pages of a magazine, but that was only because she paid one of her house-stagers from work to come and do the decorating for her. Win-win.

A tinkling bell announced Lily's entrance into the bedroom, and Alexis crouched down to give her dog some affection. "And you look perfectly festive in your red velvet collar, don't you, beautiful?" She admired the silver bell hanging from a bow and cringed at the recollection of how much this little accessory cost. "You're worth it, precious." People spent the earth on their children at Christmas. There. Totally justified. "Sorry, Miss Lily, but I have to go. I'll be home later. Don't overexert yourself."

Alexis hurried downstairs, slipped into her cream leather jacket, and inspected her reflection in the giant entryway mirror. She'd curled her long blonde locks as she was meeting a certain "John Smith" later. Black skinny jeans and a patterned blouse, black high-heeled boots and an oversized wool scarf, yes—professional but stylish. And her designer snow boots and padded jacket were in the truck, ready to wear at the cabin this afternoon. She was nothing if not practical.

The open house was at a heritage home in downtown Hollybrook, and by the time Alexis's truck warmed to a comfortable temperature, she arrived at her destination and parked the truck on the empty driveway. She knew the drill with this one since the house had been on the market for several months. The owners insisted they should give their home one more showing before their family descended upon them for Christmas, so Alexis had agreed.

The house oozed charm and was within walking distance of the main street in an appealing area of town. Not to Alexis's personal taste but delightful and well maintained. Surely, someone would fall in love with the place. *Perhaps today is the day.*

She grabbed her leather laptop bag that doubled as a purse and exited the truck. Wrapping her scarf tighter around her neck, she plucked the "Open House" sign from the back seat and planted it in a perfect mound of snow at the edge of the property. She then navigated the front path with care—at least the owners thought to clear and salt the walkway.

Alexis rang the doorbell on the off chance someone was still home and checked her watch. They should have vacated the place by now, but she never could be too sure. Spying the lockbox, she punched in her memorized code, opened the lid, and retrieved the front door key. She took one last look around outside. No one else was in sight—

perhaps the chillier temperature was keeping everyone cozy indoors this morning. *Please, let it be nice and warm inside.* Some of these heritage homes could be drafty, and not everyone had the common sense to make sure their house was set at a welcoming temperature for prospective buyers. Or bored realtors.

When Alexis unlocked the front door and stepped inside, she was relieved as immediate warmth enveloped her like a hug. She would walk the rooms to be sure everything was in order, but first, she had to set up her paperwork and business cards in the kitchen. Ever the optimist that any clients would actually show up today.

She wiped her boots on the generous-sized mat in the entrance and inhaled the subtle scent of cinnamon and apple in the air. Alexis smiled. *Nice.* The owners had taken note of her tips for a successful showing. Everything seemed tidy and clean as she made her way to the back of the home and the farmhouse-style kitchen. Her heels clip-clopped on the black-and-white tiles until she reached the kitchen island.

Alexis froze.

What? Who knew?

She set her laptop bag on the island beside a snow globe crafted from an upside-down bulbous jar. A red bow sat on top, as if it were a gift for someone. Was the snow globe for her? Would the owners have known hers smashed outside the bookstore? Word travelled fast in Hollybrook. Or maybe the gift was for someone else. Alexis couldn't resist checking a shiny tag that dangled from the ribbon and read her name, clear as day.

Alexis's heart swelled at the kind gesture. She picked up the globe to see what was depicted in the snow scene. Her broken one had a little girl with long blonde hair building a cheery snowman. It reminded her of happy winters from her childhood.

Alexis held this one at eye level. What on earth? On the snow-covered ground in this winter scene lay a miniature black gun. And beside it, the snow was stained with a tiny patch of red. Blood.

She let out a cry and slammed the globe back onto the island.

This was wrong. So wrong.

Alexis's body numbed, and the blood rushed from her head for several seconds. She grabbed her bag and clipped down the hallway. Tears blurred her eyes, and her pulse thrummed in her ears, but she had to get out of there. Now.

Steps away from the front door, she stopped. The old-fashioned handle jerked downwards, and the wooden door swung in toward her.

A man's silhouette filled the entrance.

Alexis screamed.

CHAPTER FIVE

"Alexis?" Tom raised both hands and took a step back. "It's me. Tom Harrington. John Smith?" How could he reassure her? He tugged the knitted hat from his head and pointed to the bandage on his forehead. "I'm not going to hurt you."

Alexis exhaled and leaned against a wall in the hallway. Something had spooked her. Big time.

She straightened from the wall and brushed her long, blonde hair behind her shoulders like she'd done at the hospital yesterday. "What are you doing here? You scared me to death."

"Is everything all right? You're rather pale." He was afraid to move as she looked capable of lashing out.

"How did you know I would be here?" She stood to full height.

Her blue eyes bore into his. Intelligent sparkling sapphires with a navy rim that he hadn't appreciated yesterday. Must have been the medication. How did he miss such intriguing beauty?

"Believe it or not, I didn't know you would be here until

I walked past your sign. It has your name plastered all over it, you know. And a very nice photo." He nodded over his shoulder toward the front yard.

Alexis set her jaw. "And why are you walking around down here on a freezing morning when you only got out of hospital yesterday?"

This was quite the interrogation. "My hotel is at the end of this road. I slept well, and I feel fine. I was hoping to find a decent place for coffee. Isn't this the way to the main street?" He stuffed his hands in his coat pockets and winced. The arm was still a little tender.

"I'm sorry." She shook her head and blinked several times. "I'm not usually this skittish."

Tom's stomach knotted. "Did something happen?" *Dear Lord, please don't let her get mixed up in all this.* He reached out his hand and touched her jacket sleeve. "You can tell me. I know we only just met, but I'd hate to think you were in trouble and that it might be in any way connected to the shooting."

She stared at him for what seemed like five minutes but was probably five seconds. Five very long, weighing-him-up seconds. "Close the door behind you, and come on in."

Tom shut out the cold morning air and followed her through to the back of the house, which was warm and well appointed. He appreciated older homes, especially living in an English city like Bath. This was probably classed as heritage in this infant country. In England, this house would almost be a new build.

"Delightful kitchen." Homey and bright. Lots of knotty pine combined with chic appliances. The kitchen island stole the show with a slab of what appeared to be white marble.

"Look." Alexis's shaking finger pointed at a snow globe sitting on the island.

"What do we have here? You mentioned your snow globe smashed at the ominous shooting." He went to lift the orb, and she batted his arm away. Luckily, his uninjured arm.

"Don't touch it. There may be prints."

"Excuse me?" Was this what had freaked her out? He put his hands behind his back and bent down to inspect the snow globe.

"The gift tag says it's for me." Alexis hugged her torso. "What do you think?"

"Looks homemade. But still impressive." Tom peered around a strand of the ribbon so he could study the scene inside the globe. He squinted. "Wait, a gun?" What in the world? Tom straightened. "Any idea who—"

"Nope." She hitched her bag up on her shoulder. "But I'm not sticking around to find out. If this is someone's sick idea of a joke, they'll have me to answer to." Her eyes flashed.

"And if it's... not a joke?" Tom held his breath.

She strode past him in the direction of the entrance. "Then I guess I'm in trouble." She held the front door open for him. "And as you're the one with the gunshot wound, that may mean you're in trouble, too."

Tom swallowed and pulled on his hat. "I think we should report this."

"That's my plan. I'm glad you said *we* because I have a rather possessive old flame on the police force, and I know he'll insist on speaking with you."

An old flame, hey? This woman was getting more fascinating by the minute. "Lead the way."

❄

The testosterone was palpable.

In a stuffy room in the downtown police station, Alexis glanced from Tom to David—Officer Baxter—and suppressed a grin. They'd been going at it for ten minutes, and neither man was backing down.

"And you were in this house why, exactly?" David leaned back in his office chair and narrowed his eyes at Tom.

"I was taking a walk." Tom folded his arms across his chest. "I don't believe there's a law against that."

David snorted. "Seems interesting timing to me."

"What exactly are you inferring, Officer?"

Alexis stood. "Look, David, we've reported the incident. Do you really think Tom would report something he was involved with?"

David lifted his chin. "He's an author. I'm sure he's more than capable of spinning a yarn…"

"For heaven's sake." Alexis stepped toward the closed door and turned back to Tom. "Coming?"

"If the good officer has finished grilling me?" Tom stood, and his chair scraped across the floor.

"Fine. Go. But, Alexis," David pinned her with icy eyes, "please, be careful."

Alexis didn't give him the courtesy of a reply. He wanted to place the blame on Tom, and no way was this man involved. No way. "Let's get out of here, Tom."

They hurried through the police station lobby, and Tom opened the main door onto the street to let Alexis walk through.

"Thanks." She gave a half-smile. That had been an unpleasant conversation for them both.

"Sorry if I was a bit offhand in there. He gets my goat." Tom pulled up the collar of his wool coat.

"Excuse me? He gets your *what*?"

"Gets my goat. You know, he irritates me. Knows how to push my buttons."

Alexis nodded. "Ah, yes. David Baxter is an expert in that, all right. I guess he thinks he's doing his job."

"One might say he seems infatuated by you." Tom dug his hands deep into his pockets. "I'm guessing you must have quite the history."

"That's exactly what it is. History." She stopped outside the pharmacy. "You said you needed to refill a prescription?"

"Yeah. Why don't you go on ahead to the bakery to warm up, and I'll be there in a jiffy?"

Jiffy? Cute. "Sure. I'll grab a table." Alexis tucked her chin beneath the folds of her soft scarf and hurried down the snow-covered street until the sweet aroma of cinnamon and sugar hung in the frigid air.

Angel Cakes bakery was warm and bustling as she stepped inside, but she spotted an empty, cozy corner booth and rushed over to claim it. She rubbed her chilly hands together. Why had she left her gloves in her truck? Although having coffee with the dreamy famous author hadn't exactly been in her plans for this morning. Not that she was complaining.

Her pulse sped up as she pictured his chiseled face. He was charming and delightful in every way. What was the catch? This man was too good to be true. Alexis had ogled his author photo more than once over the years on the back of his novels, and now she was hanging out with him in real life in her local bakery. Her lips twitched.

She watched as bundled-up patrons dug into delicious

pastries. How had no one recognized him so far? Although with a hat and sunglasses, even the most avid historical fiction fan would be hard-pressed to pick him out on the street.

Before Tom arrived, Alexis needed to speak with her sister. She took off her scarf, slipped the phone from her jacket pocket, and dialed.

"Alexis? We just got back to the cabin. Best snowshoeing ever. Are you still at the open house?"

"No. I can't stay long, but listen. Something strange happened. I'm fine, but I wanted to let you know—"

"What? What is it?" The wobble in Carla's voice brought back memories of the poor girl this time last year when she was dealing with that dreadful stalker–attacker. But that was all in the past...

Alexis bit her lip. Tread carefully. Keep her sister calm. "I'm safe, don't panic. I already spoke with David at the police station. It could have been some kind of sick prank, but someone left me a creepy snow globe at the open house. Had a teeny gun and everything."

Carla gasped. "Where are you now?"

"I'm at Angel Cakes, but please stay with Rhys up there at the cabin. It'll make me feel better." She forced a little extra bravado. "I'm about to have a quick coffee with Tom Harrington."

"Seriously?"

"Long story. I'll fill you in later. What time do you need me up there?"

"Umm. Mid-afternoon? But a gun in a snow globe? Was the house broken into? Lex, are you sure you're up to skating? We can postpone—"

"The police are checking the house out now. Fresh air

will do me good. You still want your first wedding dance to be on ice, right?"

"Yeah, I was hoping—"

"Well then, for the dance to be amazing, you need to practice, and we're not going to let anything stop that. I'll be a kind coach. Promise. Might as well make use of all those wretched lessons I had as a kid."

A draft of chilly air blew straight through the little bakery. Tom appeared at the entrance and slid off his sunglasses. Alexis waved.

"I have to go. Take care. See you later." She slid the phone into her pocket and watched Tom stroll toward her. He was *so* her type. Not that she was looking. When was the last time she even went on a date?

"This is a delightful place." Tom glanced around as he settled into the booth and shrugged out of his coat—not the one Alexis stroked when she thought he might be bleeding out on the snow—this one was navy wool with silver buttons. Another classy garment. Alexis tried not to stare at his dapper appearance in a black turtleneck sweater and exceedingly well-fitted dark jeans.

"Have you ordered yet?" he asked.

Alexis cleared her throat. "No, I was waiting for you. What would you like? Are you hungry?" She was not. Her stomach had been churning since she set eyes on that snow globe.

"I think I'll have a black coffee. Maybe a snack. Can you recommend anything?"

"Molly is a phenomenal baker. My favorite is her chocolate pecan caramel brownie. But she has some amazing Christmas treats, too. What are you in the mood for?" Alexis leaned an elbow on the table and rested her chin on her hand. She may have batted her lashes a little.

Tom pulled off his hat. "My sweet tooth is in fine form. Brownie sounds great."

"Let me get that ordered." Alexis waved down a teenage girl she didn't recognize. "Where's Molly?"

"Hi, she's on her break. What can I get you guys?" The server gazed over at Tom and gave him a lingering smile. Really?

Alexis jutted her chin. "Two black coffees. One chocolate pecan caramel brownie. As quick as you can."

The girl scurried off to fulfill the order.

"Hmm." Tom reclined against the dark gray leather seating and folded his arms. "Was that the ice queen making an appearance?"

Alexis sat tall. "Excuse me?"

"At the hospital, you said you had a reputation in these parts. I think you frosted over that poor girl." He stifled a chuckle.

"Whatever." She was not in the mood to discuss her reputation.

"Want to elaborate? I'm fascinated to know what makes an ice queen."

Alexis huffed. "Coming home to Hollybrook after living away for a few years was difficult. I grew up here and made some... mistakes." She tucked her hair behind her ears. "People find me prickly, and that's fine by me. I don't need them." A bare-faced lie. The loneliness was suffocating.

"Anyone? You don't need anyone?" His eyebrows drew together, puckering the square bandage on his forehead. "What about family?"

Alexis's shoulders sagged. "I only have my sister Carla here. My parents are missionaries in India."

"Really? Missionaries?" His emerald eyes gleamed. "That's amazing. I'm a Christian, too."

Oh, great. Alexis sighed. "How nice. You'll get on well with my sister. And my parents."

He squinted. "But not with you?"

The server approached their table and set everything down before them in silence.

"Thanks." Tom rewarded her with a mega-watt grin.

She didn't make eye contact with Alexis before leaving.

Tom cleared his throat. "So, you don't share your family's faith?"

Alexis refrained from rolling her eyes. Apparently, he was not going to let this God thing go. "I did when I was a kid. I guess I outgrew it." She blew on her coffee and took a tentative sip. Bitter. How fitting.

"I hear you. To be honest, I'm only recently talking to God again myself."

"Oh?"

Tom stared past her. "I got angry when my prayers weren't answered."

"Understandable." Comforting to know this man wasn't perfect.

He forked a piece of brownie into his mouth and tipped back his head. "This is heavenly." He pushed the plate into the center of their table. "Please, help yourself."

"I'm good. Thanks, though." The talk of faith curbed her appetite. "Enough about me. Tell me about you. Where do you live in England? Do you have family there?"

"I've always lived in Bath. My mum and my granny raised me on the outskirts, and then I went to University there. Now I have a flat in the center of the city. I love it. Lots of history. Decent food scene. I love my church." He winked at her.

Winked? Good grief. "And do you live... alone?" This

was Alexis's polite way of asking if he had a significant other.

"I do. Granny is close by. She's living it up in a fancy seniors' home. Honestly, she has a better social life than me." He chewed on another bite of gooey goodness and patted his mouth with a white paper napkin.

"And your mom?"

Tom folded the napkin. "Mum died. Almost a year ago. She was sick for a long time."

The unanswered prayer? "I'm so sorry."

He stared at her with glassy eyes. This was fresh grief. "Thanks. We spent a lot of time in the hospital. But I know she's with God now and is no longer in pain. That helps."

"Right." Alexis's heart melted. Peace could be found in that reassurance. She remembered when her own grandparents passed away. How she sensed hope in the loss, knowing they had gone to be with their Jesus. They had lived in the cabin where Carla and Rhys were now setting up home. Grandpa built it decades ago...

"You look miles away there."

Alexis shook her head. "I was. Listen, I'm heading to the cabin to meet Carla. Are you going to be okay to drive up? I mean, with the concussion and all."

"No problem. I got the go-ahead from the doctor."

She sipped her coffee. "Good. I'll be at your place at three o'clock to make sure everything is fabulous in your rental."

"Is my cabin really that close to your sister's place?"

Alexis pulled her scarf from the seat and wound it around her neck. "Literally on the same lake. Four or five cabins along the shore. Yours is small but cozy, and I think you'll be comfortable there."

Tom took a swig from his mug and went to stand.

"No, you stay here and take your time." Alexis nodded to the back of the bakery. "I'll pay on my way to the ladies' room. Don't even think about arguing. It's the least I can do after putting you through a grilling with Officer Baxter." A giggle slipped out.

Tom nodded. "True. He's intense. But I'm sure he's good at his job."

"He's all over the investigation, I can assure you."

"And for the record, I don't think he's over you."

Alexis stood and collected her purse. "Tell me about it. He's been in love with me since elementary school."

Tom shook his head. "Poor guy."

"Whatever. I'll see you later. In the meantime, I've got a wedding to plan..." Alexis flicked her hair over one shoulder and caught a frown on Tom's handsome face. "What's wrong?"

"Nothing. Nothing at all. Bye for now."

Weird. "Bye."

The single washroom was tiny and windowless, and Alexis shuddered at the close quarters. As she washed her hands and studied her reflection, the crow's feet wrinkling the outer edges of her eyes mocked her. Aging sucked. She would be thirty-three in April. *Thirty-three.* And still single.

Alexis held her hands under the high-powered drier that made a person's hand skin sag in the most unflattering way and let out a groan. Sagging, bagging, and flagging—was this what she had to look forward to? And all alone.

A knock on the door shook her from her daydream. Carla's wedding was messing with her head. She didn't need anyone. She was a strong, independent woman. She was happy alone. Wasn't she?

Another knock.

"Give me a minute." Alexis would take her own sweet

time, thank you. She dug her lipstick from the depths of her bag and reapplied with care. Strong, independent woman.

She swiveled from the sink, pulled down the door handle, and gave it a tug.

Nothing.

She tried again. And again. "Hey, are you holding the handle out there?" A tinge of hysteria etched her words.

"No." The muffled reply was indignant.

Alexis glanced around the cramped space and took a breath. *The door's merely stuck. Don't overreact.* She pulled the handle down slowly this time and then tugged with all her might. Still didn't budge. She was trapped, and the walls were closing in.

"Hey, can you get someone? The stupid door's stuck."

The woman on the outside grumbled. "I need to use the bathroom."

Alexis gritted her teeth. "And I need to get out of here. Go get help. *Now!*"

"Fine."

Shuffling feet faded as Alexis's heart rate sped up. Every beat reverberated in her chest. Her face heated, and she shed her scarf and dumped her bag on the floor as she paced two steps in each direction. *Breathe.* Slow, deep breaths. She knew the drill. Focus on something. Her watch. She stared at the second hand as it swept the pink pearl face with the grace of a ballerina. *Breathe.* One minute. Where was that woman? Why was it so hot in here?

"Alexis?" A male voice with an English accent stopped her mid-stride.

"Tom?" She cringed at the croak. "I'm stuck in here." Tears pooled in her eyes, and she leaned against the door, both palms against the cool, white wood. "I need to get out."

"I know. We'll have you out in a jiffy."

The jiffy again? She almost laughed. Then almost cried. Another male voice mumbled in the hallway.

"Can you stand back?" the other voice yelled.

"Yes." Alexis grabbed her scarf and bag and backed up as far as she could to the opposite wall. She inhaled and closed her eyes. Not long now. Scraping. Tapping. A drill? She flinched when the door flung open, and Tom toppled into the ladies' room.

"Thank goodness." She fell into his arms and buried her face in his black sweater. He was safe. Solid. Strong. And he smelled like cedar and bergamot...

"You're trembling." Tom pulled her close and stroked her back. "Hey, you're okay. Everything's okay."

For a moment, Alexis relished the sweet relief of freedom mingled with the thrill of his arms around her and then regained her composure and stepped back. "Sorry about that. I have to get out of here." She squeezed past Tom, an old guy, and a disgruntled gray-haired woman and took long strides through the cramped hallway into the open area of the bakery, where she grabbed the back of an empty chair and caught her breath.

The old guy followed her with a toolbox in hand. "You all right, Miss? It's Alexis, isn't it?" He furrowed his brow.

She nodded, not quite trusting her voice. Especially when Tom appeared at his side.

"Good thing I was here." The elderly man rolled up the sleeves of his red plaid shirt, revealing white hairy arms. "The wife had me working on her shelves in the kitchen."

Of course. He was Molly's husband. "Well, thanks for your help. Does that happen often? The door getting stuck? I'm a bit claustrophobic, so I'll avoid going in there in the future."

He shrugged. "Can't say it's ever happened before.

Don't know for sure, but it looked to me like someone tampered with the lock. But that's crazy." He scratched his head and ambled away with his toolbox.

"Yes, so crazy." Alexis caught Tom's eye.

A shadow of fear with a hint of guilt washed over his face. "Alexis..."

"I feel like trouble started following me around when I met you, Tom Harrington. What aren't you telling me?" She set her hands on her hips.

Tom ran his fingers over the sexy stubble beard he had going and stared at Alexis with his green eyes that reminded her of the forest in summer. "I don't know what to tell you. Truly, I don't know who has it in for me, and I don't get why you may be involved. Our paths only crossed a couple of days ago. I promise I have no intention of putting you in any danger."

"Well, that's not good enough." She checked her watch and huffed. "But I have to leave. We *will* talk later."

"Of course." Tom shook his head. "I'm sorry about all this..."

Alexis slipped her purse over her shoulder. "I'll see you at your cabin at three. Don't be late."

This man was both delicious and dangerous.

A drive up the mountain would clear her head.

And steady the erratic rhythm of her heart.

CHAPTER SIX

Tom turned the steering wheel of the rental car and grimaced. His injured arm throbbed. He considered himself a competent driver, but he'd never driven in snow before and needed to focus on the unfamiliar terrain. Add to that, he was now on the "wrong" side of the road, and yes, he had to pay extra attention.

He glanced to his right. Concentrating was easier said than done with breathtaking views of glorious mountains in the distance and snow-clad pine trees as far as the eye could see. This was like driving through the scene of a Christmas card, and the vistas got more stunning the farther he ventured from town.

His stay at the hotel was short and sweet, and so far, no one seemed to recognize Tom Harrington. That suited him perfectly; he would stick to wearing a hat and sunglasses during the day. So different from back in the UK, where he could barely get his groceries without being stopped for a selfie. His readership seemed more concentrated on that side of the pond. Made sense.

Tom peered in his rearview mirror at the town's

symmetrical grid of streets dotted with twinkling lights, now bustling with Saturday shoppers. One week until Christmas. What would the festive season be like away from home? Another first. Along with the first Christmas without his mum. A heaviness settled on his chest. *God, when will the pain of loss lessen?* Half of him was afraid of her memory fading and the other half longed to move beyond the agony.

The GPS snapped him back to the present with its Canadian accent giving directions. Tom made better time than anticipated. He would be a tad early to meet with Alexis, but that was fine. Maybe he'd take a little poke around the area, spend some time figuring out what made Miss Alexis James tick.

Back in the bakery, she mentioned in passing that she was planning a wedding. *Her* wedding? Strange after the way she was talking about not needing anyone. Didn't even mention a fiancé. Poor chump, whoever he was. And those flirtatious vibes she directed his way were subtle but present. Oh well, he'd take the attention as a compliment.

He'd been smitten with Alexis when she visited him at the hospital—they had a comfortable chemistry—not to mention the fact that she was gorgeous, strong, and... vulnerable? Maybe not at first blush, but he had a feeling this woman possessed many deep layers. Including her thoughts on God.

Shared faith was a high priority on Tom's list when it came to any serious romantic relationship. Especially now that he was back on speaking terms with God. This was all academic, of course, and he had no reason to be thinking these thoughts if Alexis was engaged to be married. *Get a grip, Tom. She's taken.*

He'd struggled with his faith journey when his mum got

sick and was furious with God for taking her so soon. Too soon. But Granny reminded him God can handle our ranting and raging. He was big enough and patient enough to take it all. And now, Tom was breaking through the surface after being submerged in frustration and fury for over a year. Most likely the reason why he failed to write anything of substance in that time. He'd been a mess.

The demanding GPS voice gave more commands, and Tom turned right at Mountain Way. The writer in him scoffed at the unimaginative street name. Then cringed at the thought of being a writer. Who was he to judge anyone with regard to creativity? He might be a best-selling author with one particular novel, *The Paris Whisperer*, which rocketed him above and beyond his wildest dreams, but had he used up every last word on that book? He'd never experienced writer's block before. Always insisted writing was a matter of sitting in the chair and doing the work.

Until now.

One more right turn, and he reached his destination. Tom slowed the car as he approached several cabins and pulled in beside a frozen lake. He leaned forward over the steering wheel and took in the storybook scene before him. The collection of cabins, assorted in size and style, appeared to gather in a huddle to stay warm in this clearing of snowy pine trees, except for the fire was water. Or ice.

Tom counted maybe a dozen log homes, most topped with a puff of pale gray smoke curling into the turquoise cloudless sky. Beyond the plethora of trees, mountains stretched lazily as if they had nothing to do but look majestic all day long. Idyllic. And perhaps the perfect place to get creative and break out of this writing funk.

"Hello there."

Tom startled as a middle-aged woman bundled in snow gear knocked on his window.

"Are you lost, dear?" She pulled her scarf down and offered a smile.

Tom lowered the window. "Afternoon. I'm looking for number..." He consulted his phone. "Number seven, Clearwater Crescent."

"Number seven? Are you renting?"

He nodded. "Yes, I'm here for a month."

"And you're English?" She clapped her mittens together. "How perfect. Is it only you?" She eyed the empty back seat.

Tom smirked. "Umm, thanks. And yes. Only me. Could you point out number seven?"

"Of course." The friendly neighbor bent over to his eye level and gestured around the corner to the smallest cabin in the huddle. "Red front door. And if you need anything, you come to number eleven. I'm Hattie, and you can borrow a cup of sugar from me anytime."

"That's very kind. Thank you, Hattie. Enjoy your walk."

"I will. What was your name, dear?"

"Umm, John."

Tom closed the window before she could interrogate him further. John Smith was the name he used on the rental agreement, so in this neighborhood, he should stick with that name for as long as possible. He shivered as he drove around the perimeter of the lake. The temperature was colder at this elevation. He would have to harden up if he intended to embrace the great outdoors, like Hattie.

"Number seven." Tom eyed the cozy A-frame with the scarlet front door. Far enough from the homes on either side to afford him the privacy and peace he craved, yet close enough to remind him of his need for community. As an introvert, his preference was to hole up and hunker down, particularly when in the midst of a writing project.

Please, Lord, let this place give me inspiration to even find a writing project...

He was desperate to move on from this no man's land where he failed to find a footing in his writing, his relationships, and his future in general. Everything was up for grabs.

Faith.

The word echoed in his soul.

I know, I know. Tom turned off the ignition and checked the time. Ten minutes to spare before Alexis showed. Might as well bundle up and take a look around outside. He slipped on the overpriced jacket he purchased online for his time in the mountains, taking care with his bandaged, tender upper arm. Ski gloves, cashmere scarf, and his woolen hat that covered his other bandage, and he was set.

Tom exited the car and raised his face toward the clear sky. Despite the chill in the air, the sun kissed his cheeks with warmth as he soaked in the rays through limited inches of exposed skin. Maybe he needed the nourishment of sunshine. Or the pure, clean oxygen only found on a pristine mountain.

The sound of women's voices broke his moment of solitude, and he trudged in his new snow boots along the side of the cabin toward the lake, the crunch beneath his feet oddly satisfying. He ran a gloved hand along the caramel-colored logs that encased his new home-away-from-home, and when he reached the backyard, he grinned.

"I'd forgotten about this little perk." A small, covered hot tub squatted on an elevated deck and beckoned his cold, aching limbs. Being shot had taken its toll on his body, and the notion of relaxing in bubbly jets of hot water sounded like perfection. "Don't worry, I'll be making good use of you."

Tom wandered to the edge of the frozen lake and lowered himself onto one of two red Adirondack chairs. If he had to wait around for a few minutes, this seemed like the ideal spot.

A woman's laughter drew his gaze to the right, and when he leaned forward, he spotted two figures out on the ice. Were they skating? And the blonde looked like... yes, that had to be her. Alexis. Different jacket than she had worn earlier, but that was her, for sure. She mentioned her sister lived here. Maybe the shorter brunette was the sister. He was no skating expert, but they appeared to be dancing. Impressive.

As curious as he was, Tom averted his eyes and pulled out his phone. He had promised himself not to allow the device to be the boss on this trip, but he had to see if Granny had left any messages. Or if he'd received any news on the shooting. There'd been nothing since Thursday evening, although the snow globe fiasco this morning was suspicious—unless Alexis was mixed up in troubles of her own.

Of course, no Wi-Fi. The cabin description claimed to provide decent connection, so he'd have to wait until Alexis let him inside. Unless she'd left a key somewhere. A chill shuddered through his entire body, so he pocketed the phone and stood. Keep moving. These temperatures were not for the weak. He glanced once more at the lake, and Alexis swirled into a pirouette move that caused the other skater to cheer and his own jaw to drop. This woman was something else.

Retracing his footprints in the snow, Tom plodded to the red front door with its welcome mat announcing *Home Sweet Home*. He checked underneath the mat in case a key was hidden there, but he came up empty. Next to the door, a black metal mailbox was attached to the log siding. Tom reached his hand inside and ran his fingers around. Something.

He tugged off his glove and delved back in to retrieve a gleaming silver key. *Bingo.* "Well, that was easy."

Alexis should be here soon. Should he wait? The cabin could be fitted with an alarm. Tom racked his brains but didn't recall any mention of an alarm system. The neighborhood seemed close-knit up here. Worst case scenario, the alarm would start, and Alexis would hustle on over. Tom needed Wi-Fi and more pain meds, and if he were honest, his whole body was freezing. More power to Hattie.

Tom inserted the key and turned. So far, so good. He stomped his snowy boots and stepped inside onto another larger mat. His cheeks warmed, and the absence of an obnoxious beep was a huge relief. He looked back at the car. He'd wait for Alexis before bringing in his stuff. Let her do the tour and whatnot. He only needed a glass of water for the pills in his pocket and to try his phone again. The Wi-Fi code was usually posted somewhere obvious in these rental places.

He struggled out of his boots and left them on a rubber tray near the door before getting his bearings. The comforting smell of cedar filled his senses. And even from the entrance, the panoramic view of the lake through the wall of windows at the back of the home invited him far beyond the glass.

"Very nice indeed."

The open-plan area incorporated a modernized black

and white kitchen and a cozy living room, separated by a long, sleek island. Black leather sofas, lots of red plaid cushions and blankets, and a wood-burning fireplace. Even a decorated Christmas tree glowed in the corner. But that view of lake and mountains, white on white—it was nothing short of glorious.

Tom pulled off his hat and caught the edge of the bandage. Ouch. *Hope that didn't mess with the stitches.* He was ready for his painkillers; he'd timed it so he would be clear-headed for the drive, but now he had no intention of going anywhere. Except maybe the hot tub waiting for him on the deck.

He unzipped his jacket and dug into his pocket for the medication as he hummed a carol and plodded over to the kitchen. A glass of water, and maybe then he'd scour the cupboards for tea. A rectangular file on the kitchen island caught his eye, most likely the house rules and Wi-Fi code. But as he approached, lying on top of the file was a sheet of paper. No, a book cover.

His book cover. *How curious.* He flipped it over.

The bottle of pills slid from Tom's grip and clattered to the floor.

CHAPTER SEVEN

Alexis spotted a car, presumably Tom Harrington's rental, in the driveway of number seven. She groaned. He was early. She always prided herself on being punctual, and now she was two minutes late because Carla insisted on them nailing the ending to her wedding dance on the ice. She squinted. He wasn't in the driver's seat. And not a soul was in sight. Had the cheeky Englishman found the key and gone inside? Her face heated as she stomped to the front door. She already planned to grill him about this morning. This added fuel to her fire.

"Tom?" Alexis used her strictest voice as she entered the darling cabin. A large pair of boots took up space on the tray. She slipped off her own and dumped them next to his. "Thanks for waiting." He was British. He would comprehend sarcasm.

Tom stood with his back to her, gazing through the glass French doors. Admittedly, the lake view was stunning, but how rude.

"Tom."

He swiveled around and almost dropped his phone.

"Sorry." He pulled a pair of earbuds from his ears. "Didn't hear you come in."

Alexis planted a hand on her hip. "Umm, can I ask why you're in here already? You were supposed to wait for me."

He didn't look well. Face pinched, shoulders hunched.

"Hey, are you alright?" Alexis dumped her bag on the kitchen island and dashed over to him, her anger forgotten. "Sit down for a minute; you don't look too good." To be fair, the guy had been in hospital the previous day. She led him to one of the couches and helped him out of his ski jacket. "Let me get you some water."

"Thanks." Tom rubbed at his cheeks as if to revive himself. "Were you in here earlier?"

"Today? No. I haven't been inside for a while. I guess the cleaning service came in either yesterday or this morning. Is there a problem?" She located the glassware and poured them both a drink from the water button on the fridge. She was parched after skating.

"I was curious about the key in the mailbox, that's all. Is security not an issue here?" He placed his phone on the wooden coffee table and accepted the offered glass. "Thanks."

Alexis perched on the arm of the opposite sofa and drained half her water. "I popped the key in the mailbox before I went to my sister's place. It really is safe up here, and the road doesn't lead anywhere else. The neighbors are extra vigilant." She bit her lower lip. "There was a whole thing last Christmas at my sister's cabin—please don't ask, it's a long story—but that was all resolved, and now the locals don't even bother locking their doors half the time."

"Right." He stared into his glass.

"The neighborhood is pretty remote. But are you worried?" Something had shaken him.

"No, not at all." His smile failed to hide the tightness in his eyes. "Need my pain meds to kick in and maybe a nap. Don't mind me."

She tilted her head. "Are you sure you're good?"

"Positive. And it's me who should be asking *you* after the stressful morning you had." He rested his forearms on his knees. "Did you hear any more about the snow globe mystery?"

Alexis's skin prickled. "Yeah. The open house was broken into sometime after the owners left and before I arrived. They've been questioned and were shocked about the whole thing. The snow globe wasn't there when they left the house, and the backdoor lock had been tampered with."

"Oh." He swallowed. "Like in the bakery. Rather a coincidence, don't you think?"

"I don't know what to think." Could anything else possibly go wrong today?

"Getting stuck in that bathroom freaked you out. Are you claustrophobic?"

An understatement. "A bit. No biggie." A change of subject was in order. "Can I ask you a weird question?"

Tom sipped his water. "Fire away."

"Do you think I look like the woman on the front cover of your book?"

He set his glass down on the table with a thud. "You mean on *The Paris Whisperer?*"

Alexis nodded.

"Why do you ask?" Tom scraped a hand through his hair.

"Something my sister said. No need to get touchy. I mean, it's not a criticism or anything..."

"No, no. Of course not. Sorry." Tom studied her hair

and her face. "Yes, I suppose you do. I did think that briefly when I first saw you in the hospital. Different color eyes."

"Observant."

He shrugged one shoulder. "Paying attention is my job. The character was birthed from my imagination, and I could tell you everything about her. And she had chocolate brown eyes."

"Brown." Alexis nodded. "Got it."

"Any particular reason you wanted to know?"

Alexis gazed out over the frozen lake. "After Carla mentioned the cover, I checked online, and I have to say, there's a resemblance. What are the chances?"

Tom frowned. "Has anyone else mentioned it? The resemblance?"

"I don't think so."

"Good."

She squinted. "Good?"

He cracked his knuckles. "I mean, the last thing you need is for people to put you and me together thinking you're my girl from the book cover. Especially as someone tried to shoot me. Not that anyone has recognized me so far. At least, I don't think so. But I don't want to put a target on your back. And I understand if you'd rather keep your distance. Not that there's anything else going on between us." He winced. "I'm rambling."

"No kidding." *A target on my back?* What was he talking about? Alexis placed her glass on the coffee table. "And for the record, it's nobody else's business whom I choose to spend time with."

Tom smirked. "Is that right?"

"Absolutely." She folded her arms across her chest. "I refuse to let the stupid snow globe incident ruin my life. Someone's idea of a sick joke. I haven't got time for that."

Not until after the wedding. *I can't ruin this special week for my little sister.*

"Is your friend at the police station concerned?" A glint shone in his green irises. Was he teasing her?

"David? He's always concerned. Don't worry about him." She got up and sauntered over to the kitchen and collected the tan leather folder holding all the information he would require during his stay. "But I'm a grown woman, and I can look after myself."

"Yes. I can see that."

Alexis joined him on the couch and handed over the folder. "All the phone numbers you may need during your stay are here. The Wi-Fi code. It can be spotty, but they have the best possible option in this cabin. Local attractions if you get bored. Shopping, entertainment, churches. All listed."

"Do you have a church you can recommend?" His eyes twinkled with mischief. Was he baiting her?

"No. I can ask my sister."

"What about the church for the wedding?" He ran his fingers through the top of his dark hair—it was almost jet-black in this light. Glossy. Touchable.

"The wedding is at my sister's cabin." Why did he have to keep on about the church stuff? His hair was terribly distracting.

"I saw you skating." He nodded at the windows. "You're good."

"Thanks. I had lessons as a kid." *Back when I was popular.* "It's one of the ways I let off steam these days. Do you skate?"

He guffawed. "Gosh, no. I've been maybe three times in my entire life, and I was a disaster. Zero coordination."

"I could teach you. We have spare skates. I'm heading

back now if you want me to take you for a spin on the ice." Having him hang on to her for dear life wouldn't be horrible.

"I think not." Was he blushing? "My arm. Gunshot wound, you know."

Alexis narrowed her eyes. "Your slight graze has suddenly morphed into a full-fledged wound, has it? Perhaps I'll get you out on the ice when you've convalesced." She stood and retrieved her bag from the kitchen. "I'm going to be around a lot this week with the wedding and all, so don't be a stranger, okay? You have my card. Call if you need anything or if you have any questions. Want me to show you upstairs before I go?"

Tom stood and walked her to the front door. "I think I can figure out which is the bedroom and which is the bathroom, but thanks."

She slipped on her boots and then looked him in the eye. "I'm not sure I like the idea of you being a hermit in here. Especially given the fact you were shot, whether it was random or intentional. Keep your phone on. If we make any plans for this evening, I'll give you a shout."

Tom broke eye contact and shuffled his feet. "That's kind, but I don't want to intrude."

"Are you kidding me? Carla's desperate to meet you. She may even be a bigger fan than me." She gave a wink. "Enjoy your nap."

Alexis hurried past his car and around the lake to Carla's cabin. A nap sounded tempting. Maybe she'd have time before her sister called her back out on the ice. Since when had Carla become the bossy one?

Poor Tom, he seemed frazzled. Was he nervous about the lack of security? He'd been shot at. That was enough for anyone to need some major counseling sessions. She glanced around at the winter wonderland. The area was deserted. She wasn't the nervous type, and this lake was like her second home, but the shooting and the snow globe incident had to be connected. She picked up her pace. Another conversation with Tom might bring clarity.

❄

Tom unpacked the last of his clothes into the spacious upstairs closet and flopped onto the bed. At least it was comfortable. And his arm wasn't bugging him anymore. He turned on his side and looked through the window at the lake. What this cabin lacked in size it made up for with the view. The only place he couldn't see the lake was from the bathroom, and even that was luxurious with its clawfoot tub and small steam shower.

Movement out on the ice. Tom pushed himself up to see if it might be Alexis. It was. That woman had energy. After the drama this morning at the open house and the bakery, she was still going strong. From what she said earlier, she would soon be married at her sister's cabin. That was the main reason why he couldn't tell her about the book cover he found in the kitchen. How could he add to her stress the week she was getting married? Perhaps he could talk to the sister instead. Or should he call that police officer and try not to sound unhinged?

Alexis was a conundrum. Tom didn't like to pepper her with questions, but he was fascinated. He let out a sigh. She was still sending an occasional flirty vibe his way, but perhaps he was reading too much into it. Seeing her with the man she was about to marry may help quash his attraction to the woman. Because he wasn't imagining the gleam in her eye when she looked at him. He was at risk of melting beneath her warm gaze...

Lord, help a man out here? What's happening?

Tom watched Alexis's graceful figure glide in large circles on the ice. She was joined by a man on skates. Must be the fiancé. Tom squinted but couldn't make much out other than an athletic build and the fact that he was rather a wobbly skater.

A tightness spread across his chest. Jealousy? That was ridiculous. The shorter brunette joined them, and the guy lifted the sister and kissed her on the mouth. What? Tom tried not to stare but couldn't tear his gaze away. Now, a second male joined them. What was with all these skating Canadians? This bloke paired off with Alexis and was a brilliant skater. He sped and flipped and oozed confidence. Tall guy, too. In fact, he looked very much like... yes, that could be Officer Baxter. David. But wasn't he the ex?

Tom rolled onto his back. This was confusing. Perhaps instead of his usual historical fiction, he should write a romance novel instead. Try to follow what was going on with the love interests on the ice. Or a thriller this time. Try to make head or tail of this situation with the snow globe and the messages.

Tom took the book cover from the pocket of his jeans and unfolded it. Was Alexis in trouble because she resembled this girl? That was nonsensical. Who was following him? Had they been on the same flight all the way from England? Known his itinerary? So many questions. This trip was not turning out the way he planned. He had not planned to meet Alexis. But he was drawn to her in a way he couldn't describe, even as a wordsmith. Maybe because she was the first one to attend to him after he was shot. They had a connection.

But Alexis had nothing to do with the reason why he was in Hollybrook. Perhaps God planned for them to meet. Their first encounter happened outside the Happily Ever After bookstore, of all places. As much as the idea pained him, he would have to find some way to explain the truth to her. What he knew of it, at least.

Tom folded up the book cover and shoved it back inside his pocket.

Alexis had a wedding to think about, and this situation was the last thing she needed to be burdened with a week before Christmas... yet surely, she must be confused by what was going on.

Tom closed his eyes. Confusion he could live with. But the snow globe had been a warning, and this book cover featuring the dead ringer for Alexis—that implied he was not the only one in imminent danger.

CHAPTER EIGHT

"I'm done." Alexis caught her breath and balanced on one skate as she headed for the bench at the edge of the frozen lake. Daylight was fading fast, along with her energy.

"You're magnificent on the ice." David Baxter landed on the bench next to her, his ruddy face way too close to hers.

Alexis scooted along, creating a reasonable space between them. "If you're hunting for a compliment back, forget it."

David knew he was an excellent skater by the numerous offers he received for ice hockey scholarships back in the day. His infatuation with her was as blatantly obvious as his skating skills, and she would not fuel that monster.

Carla collapsed on the snow beside the bench. "Thanks, sis. You're a miracle worker." She untied her laces. "We might actually be half-decent on Saturday."

Rhys dropped down next to Carla. "You're going to look sensational, honey. I'm the doofus who follows you around on the ice like a long-legged puppy."

Carla kissed him on the lips. "I think you're perfect."

"Save the mushy stuff for the big day, guys." Alexis exchanged her skates for her boots. "You'll both be fine. Everyone loves you, and they won't be expecting the bride and groom to take their first dance on the ice. It's going to be a fabulous surprise."

"Well, thanks for your patience. All of you." Rhys chuckled. "David, you sure showed me what I'm *supposed* to look like out there. Some of us weren't raised on skates."

"Not a problem." David gave him a high-five.

Alexis glanced in the direction of number seven. "Maybe Tom should come and watch you, Rhys. He needs to know we aren't all pros around here. I think he feels a bit intimidated."

"Tom Harrington?" David scowled. "What's he got to do with anything?"

Alexis's initial instinct was to lash out, but she squelched her over-reactive habit and kept her voice even. "Last time I checked, David, you weren't privy to my business."

Carla stood and pulled Rhys up to join her. "We'll head inside and get the hot chocolate going."

"Right behind you." Alexis collected her skates.

David touched her gloved hand. "Can we talk?"

"You have exactly one minute."

David ran a hand down his face. "I know you don't like being told what to do, but you need to be careful with this Harrington guy."

"I can—"

"You can look after yourself. Yes, you make that abundantly clear all the time. But there's something fishy about him—this big-time author, according to the internet—

arriving in our sleepy little town at Christmas and getting shot."

"You can't blame him for being in the wrong place at the wrong time." Alexis ground her teeth. "Maybe it was a deranged super-fan that shot at him. It happens. People do crazy things. You should be watching out for him. Doing your job."

David's shoulders sagged beneath his fitted ski jacket. "My concern is for you, Alexis. The shooting. The snow globe. What's next?"

Alexis bit her lip. She would refrain from sharing about the bakery bathroom debacle.

David put a hand on her knee. "Let me protect you." His voice was soft now. Alexis had to strain to hear him. "Let me love you. We could be as happy as Carla and Rhys. I know we could."

She leveled a stare. Why couldn't this man find himself a good, sweet, kind little woman? "What are you talking about? We gave our relationship a whirl, and it was a disaster. I'm too much for you. I'm not what you want, and deep down, you know it."

His brown eyes pooled. "That was five years ago. We've both changed. Grown. All I've ever wanted is you, Alexis. Since I was—"

"Stop." She stood, and his hand dropped to his side. "Stop. I don't know how else to tell you we're never going to be together. Ne-ver. And I'm not getting married. E-ver."

David stood and towered over her. His jaw was set, and his lips flattened. "Don't say I didn't give you a chance at happiness. I'm the only one who sticks up for you in this town. Protects your messed-up reputation. Remembers what you were like before you became *used goods*. Before you were cold-hearted and hard as granite." He grabbed his skates from the bench.

His harsh—but truthful—words were like a punch to her stomach. She almost doubled over but instead squared her shoulders. "I don't need your protection." She turned her back on him and stomped through the snow toward Carla's cabin.

"You can't stop me from doing my job." His voice carried on the frigid air as she left him behind.

Alexis blew out a ragged breath and wiped tears from her cheeks before they turned to ice.

Like the rest of her.

❄

Tom checked his reflection in the hallway mirror and grimaced. Even a trim to his neat beard and a decent nap this afternoon hadn't helped. He looked decidedly haggard. His skin was sallow with dark shadows beneath his eyes, and the wretched bandage covering half his forehead did him no favors.

"Oh, well." Granny always said he was too vain for his own good.

Bundled up and ready to walk over to Alexis's sister's cabin, he locked the door and tucked the key in his jacket pocket. The cold air took his breath away, and he buried his chin deeper beneath his scarf as he passed the parked car.

The phone call from Alexis was a lovely surprise—he hadn't expected her to offer to spend her Saturday evening with him. The invitation was to hang out around the bonfire, although he wasn't sure who would be there altogether. He switched on the powerful flashlight she reminded him to bring along and followed the snow-covered road back the way he had driven earlier, his pace brisk. The night was chilly, and he was a little concerned about what might be lurking in the way of wildlife. Meeting a bear wasn't on his bucket list, although they would all be hibernating. Right? Hibernating or hungry. Preferably the former.

Tonight, Tom would be experiencing his first s'mores, and as he had a quintessential English sweet tooth, the treat sounded like something he had to try at least once. He'd picked up a few groceries on his way out of town, and earlier on, he managed to bake a frozen pizza without too much trouble. Cooking was not his thing. But at least he wouldn't be ravenous on the off-chance these s'mores were a disappointment.

Security lights beamed as he trudged past a large modern home with a barking dog making its presence known behind a front window. Tom waved at the dog with his good arm and kept going, speeding up a little as the biting cold penetrated his layers. As chilled to the bone as he was, this walking in a winter wonderland was an experience he would remember. Maybe even write about.

Now that the dog had calmed down, the only sound was his footsteps crunching on packed snow. The trees around him, heavy with white, seemed to hold their breath. The world was hushed here. The clean air was tinged with smoke, perhaps from festive gatherings around fireplaces or Alexis's outdoor bonfire.

Paying attention was something he tried to be intentional about as a writer. Details could be missed, even by him in the hurry of everyday routines. But this was far from his everyday rhythm. This was... nostalgic somehow, even though he'd never experienced anything like it before. He shook his head to clear his musings. He was nearing the destination. Number two.

He slowed his steps and his heart rate. Breathless and out-of-shape was not a cool look on a man who was not quite thirty-five. He glanced up at the cabin. Each home dotted around the lake emanated its own personality. This cabin was loved, he could tell. He was about to knock on a blue door wearing a huge holly wreath when Alexis yelled from the lake side of the home.

"Hey, Tom. You found us. You want to come around the back? Or do you need to warm up inside for a bit?"

"I'll come around. Be right there." Tom shivered and navigated his way around a shoveled path to the rear of the property.

"Welcome." Alexis rewarded him with a beautiful smile. "You must be freezing. Let's get you by the fire." She grabbed his hand, which was numb in spite of the glove, and led him to the most charming fire pit he'd ever seen.

"This is fantastic." Tom turned off his flashlight. The deck was a mass of twinkling white lights and even boasted a decorated Christmas tree and furniture, creating a cozy place to sit and chill. Quite literally, it would seem.

"Lovely, isn't it? Have a seat. The others will be out in a sec." Alexis gestured to one of the Adirondack chairs circled around a roaring fire, and they both sat. Small wooden tree stump tables were situated beside the chairs, and again, twinkly lights wound around trees, so the area was fully lit.

His insides warmed. "It's like Santa's grotto or something."

A door creaked, and Tom turned to the cabin as the brunette and a young man appeared.

"Hi, you must be Tom." The woman was pretty, with

wavy hair down to her waist and bright red glasses. "I'm Carla. Alexis's sister. It's so lovely to meet you."

Tom stood and waited for them to navigate a few steps carrying trays of food.

Carla set down her tray and shook his hand. "I'm just going to get it out there. I'm a huge fan. Read all your books." Her cheeks glowed, and she slid an arm around the waist of the guy standing next to her.

"Hey, man. I'm Rhys. And I have a feeling I'll be reading all your books very soon." He deposited his tray on a stump and reached one hand out to Tom.

Tom appreciated the firm shake. "Well, it's awfully kind of you to invite me over. Thanks very much."

"Inviting you over is the least we could do." Carla winced. "I can't believe you were shot outside our Hollybrook bookstore. It's not how we usually like to welcome our visitors."

Tom shook his head. "The incident wasn't as bad as it appeared. Really."

"We're glad to hear that and relieved no one else was hurt." Rhys kissed Carla's cheek. "Okay, I'm on drinks duty, and the kettle's boiling. Hot chocolate or tea for you, Tom?"

"Hot chocolate sounds perfect, thanks." Hot anything would hit the spot.

"I'll be right back." Rhys disappeared, and Alexis deposited a thick blanket on each chair.

"In case you're cold." She winked at Tom. "I know you're not used to the snow."

Great. Fragile British Syndrome. "Thanks."

"So, did you manage to take a nap this afternoon? It's been eventful these past few days." Alexis crossed her long legs and snuggled into her blanket.

"I did, yes. I also spoke with my granny and sent her

some photos of my view. And then I managed to not entirely burn a frozen pizza. That's quite a success story for me."

Carla chuckled. "We all feel a little inferior in the kitchen with Rhys around. Don't worry about it."

"Oh? Is your boyfriend a good cook?"

"He's a chef. Trained in France. And he's going to be my husband a week from today. How lucky am I?" Carla put her hands on her cheeks. "I can hardly wait."

Tom frowned and looked from one sister to the other. "Wait. Are you telling me you're both getting married at the same time?"

Alexis snorted. "Me? Married? You've got to be kidding. What on earth makes you think I'm getting married?"

A rush of relief escaped Tom's lips. He hid it with a nervous chuckle. "Must have got the wrong end of the stick when you said you had a wedding to plan. I presumed you meant your own." Maybe he could talk with her about the mysterious book cover after all.

"That's too funny." Carla's face lit up. "It's definitely me getting married, though. Alexis is the most organized person I know, and so I happily handed my big day over to my big sis. She's a genius. It's going to be gorgeous."

Alexis batted away the compliment with her hand like she would a pesky gnat. "You could have done it yourself just fine. Only I'm not exactly afraid to be—"

"Bossy?" Carla lifted a brow.

"I was going to say confident, but whatever. I get things done."

"That you do." Rhys returned with another tray of four huge mugs. "I hope you're good with whipped cream, Tom?"

"I can be persuaded." Tom reached for a mug. "Thanks. This is great."

"My pleasure. So, tell me, do you have a girl back in England?"

"Rhys." Carla's jaw dropped. "That's awfully personal, considering we've only just met the poor guy."

Rhys winked. "I figured as we're doing s'mores together, we're now good friends. There's something very intimate about talking around a bonfire."

"He has a point." Tom blew on the steam rising up from his drink. "Camp conversations around the fire. That's actually when I became a Christian as a teen."

"No way." Carla's eyes sparkled. "That's fantastic."

Alexis groaned. "But back to the original awkward question..."

Tom looked around at all three of them. "I'm very much free and single." Was his imagination playing tricks, or did Alexis's mouth curve into a smile behind her mug? "The only woman in my life is my sweet Granny." He took a sip of his drink. "And it has to be said, your hot chocolate is even better than hers, and that's saying something."

"The hot chocolate is homemade because it's Rhys," Alexis teased.

Rhys stuck out his tongue. "You have to allow me this indulgence. The s'mores stuff is all prepackaged."

"My hips are going to hate you for this." Alexis patted her sides.

Those hips looked good to Tom.

"It's Christmas." Rhys winked. "Food and family in abundance. Do you have siblings, Tom?"

"What's with the inquisition, Rhys?" Alexis sent a glare across the fire pit.

"Oh, I don't mind." Warmth from the mug heated

through Tom's gloves, and he could feel his fingers again. "No siblings. I'm an only child."

"Same." Rhys handed him a plate with an assortment of ingredients. "Fixings for s'mores."

"Thanks. You're going to have to talk me through this. I'm a newbie." Tom studied the fat marshmallows, generous pieces of chocolate, and square biscuits similar to the ones Granny liked with her tea. "The only thing I've ever cooked in a bonfire is sausages with my best mate, Uri, when we were teens."

Alexis tilted her head. "That's an unusual name."

"Uriah." Tom looked over at Rhys. "He was the closest thing I had to a brother."

"Are you still close?" A line formed between Alexis's eyebrows.

Tom lowered his gaze. "We drifted apart after University. He got in with a... different crowd. We'd always planned on writing books together, actually. Collaborating and co-writing. Never came to anything, though."

Rhys zipped up his jacket. "Unlucky for him, seems to me. I guess we all have our regrets from our younger years."

"Do we ever." Alexis stared into the fire.

"Here, Tom, have a stick." Carla passed him a long, skinny branch with a sharp end. "Whittled by my own fair hand."

Tom glanced from the stick to the chocolate. This was above his culinary prowess.

Alexis chuckled. "It won't hurt you." She drew her chair up against his so their arms touched.

A shiver of desire deeper than the cold winter air ran through Tom's body.

"Spear your marshmallow." Alexis demonstrated and then leaned forward and held one end of the stick while the marshmallow end went into the fire. "You can decide how toasted you want it to be. The ideal is golden brown enough on the outside that the inside goes soft and gooey."

"Got it." Tom followed suit. "Although I do have a reputation for cooking everything very, very well done."

Alexis bumped his shoulder with hers and grinned. The firelight turned her blue eyes almost green. She pulled her hat down over her ears with one hand and studied her marshmallow in the fire. "Pay attention now."

Oh, I am. And now that Tom knew Alexis was not about to get married, his heart was melting along with his marshmallow.

CHAPTER NINE

The next morning, Alexis rolled out of bed after sleeping in an extra hour. This past week had been draining, and the following one was shaping up to be grueling physically and emotionally. House guests, the wedding, and Christmas. Not to mention the growing knot in her stomach brought on by the shooting she witnessed, the notion that someone could be watching her, the argument with David yesterday, and the unsettling presence of Tom Harrington.

"Tom."

She liked the way his name rolled off her tongue.

She liked a great deal about this Englishman who had landed smack dab in the middle of her life and disrupted her no-nonsense, workaholic tendencies.

Alexis slipped on a warm robe and padded down to the empty kitchen. Carla was at church, and rhythmical snores reverberated from the living room where Lily was taking her own day of rest. Coffee. Alexis needed coffee. And maybe she'd go crazy and enjoy a croissant with jam. Carla had left one out for her, and to not indulge would be rude. She would follow the pastry with a workout. Zero guilt.

As Alexis prepped the coffee machine, her stomach tied in knots at the memory of last night's bonfire. Her skinny cappuccino took a back burner to the heat blazing in her cheeks at the mere thought of a certain someone.

Tom told them he was single. Free. She'd felt the tingle right down to her boot-clad toes at the news. She'd learned the hard way that one could never assume a guy was unattached when he showed you attention.

The four of them stayed up way too late, but nobody had been in a rush for their time to end. Tom fit right in. When had she ever been this comfortable with a man?

And then, the way he lingered when the two of them said good night—he was respectful, even though she recognized his desire to kiss her. They had hugged, perhaps a beat longer than necessary, leaving the promise of more to come.

The steam wand whistled and then bubbled as the milk heated and frothed. Her insides did likewise.

Could Tom see through the glass shield she set in place years ago? The barrier that protected her heart and kept out the pain—but also the love. She lived in her very own version of a snow globe, where others could look in, even shake her a little, but all they could see was the perfect scene. If only they knew.

She poured the hot milk into a snowflake mug. The aroma of dark roast espresso filled the room as she added the stream of coffee in a happy swirl. The first sip was always the best. Alexis clutched the mug with both hands and blinked. Divine.

Tom wasn't intimidated by her like some men were. Perhaps because he'd only known her for a handful of days

—or perhaps because he didn't know her colorful past. But he respected her; a woman recognized these things. And those emerald eyes hinted at something deeper. He might be a perfect English gentleman, but an undeniable chemistry sizzled between them.

The way Tom had gazed at her in the glow of the fire and then laughed at himself when he got melted marshmallow over his jeans. His deep, mellow voice and humble attitude despite his fame. He paid complete attention to her when she spoke and was gentle and considerate every time their hands happened to touch—all these little moments made her feel... safe. Seen. Special.

Alexis's stomach gurgled. She pulled a knife from the drawer and a pot of jam from the fridge. Perching on the stool, she slathered the croissant and took delight in each flaky, buttery mouthful. An extra ten minutes on her elliptical would help nullify the damage. She licked the last remnants of raspberry jam from her fingers. Yes, staying on top of balancing career, exercise, and health was a constant challenge, and she mastered them all—but at the expense of relationships. And her spiritual life.

Carla's brown leather Bible on the kitchen counter caught Alexis's eye as she sipped her coffee. Carla must have forgotten to take it to church. Last night, Rhys invited Tom to join them for the service and even offered to give him a ride into town, as Rhys was already living up in the cabin. The guys bonded, for sure. Cabin neighbors. Both lacked siblings. The two of them loved all things Paris. Their faith was a big deal to them. She chuckled. Quite the bromance.

Truth be told, that was the only part of last night at the bonfire that burned for Alexis. The other three started in on their faith stories and raved about how God had helped them, and then, of course, Carla shared the love story of how God brought her and Rhys together again five years after they had broken up.

Alexis groaned. She knew all the Jesus things. She was raised by missionary parents, for goodness' sake.

So why did God feel so distant and make her feel so damaged?

That's not My voice you're hearing, daughter...

Alexis shook her head. What was that? Almost audible. Yet familiar somehow. She twisted the silver ring on her pinkie, the ring her parents bought her when she turned twelve. In her childhood, she was convinced God whispered comforting words in her ear. Especially when fear edged in and she was in small spaces and panic tickled her senses. She'd also heard Him in her lonely teens when she'd replaced friendships by hooking up with boys. But at some point, His whispers stopped. Had she drowned them out in adulthood with her relentless striving after success and status?

Curiosity got the better of her, and she pulled Carla's well-loved Bible next to her coffee mug. She hadn't cracked open one of these in years. "Let's see what my little sister's been reading." Alexis let the pages fall open where Carla had placed a handmade bookmark created by a child, decorated with brightly colored sunshine and love hearts. Most likely from the Mexican orphanage she'd been working at for the past few years.

The book of Ezekiel. Vaguely familiar, as she'd memorized the books of the Bible as a kid. One verse was highlighted in yellow. Alexis picked up her mug and read the words aloud:

"I will give you a new heart and put a new spirit in you;

I will remove from you your heart of stone and give you a heart of flesh." Ezekiel 36:26

Alexis's hand trembled, and she set the mug down before any coffee spilled on the Bible. Did she have a heart of stone? Some called her an ice queen, and she went out of her way to personify the label, but truly, the words cut deep. In her weakest moments, the loneliness was more suffocating than any elevator or tiny room. Was her actual heart cold as ice, hard as stone? Not always. But her time away from Hollybrook had changed her.

The few years she spent in Vancouver had been her undoing and her rebuilding. She'd gone there as a whip-smart business student ready to shake the carefree bad girl reputation and the Hollybrook dust off her feet and succeed in the big city. Start fresh. But she had let down her guard, fallen in love, invested emotionally and financially—and then someone took advantage of her in every way possible. She chose to reinvent herself and returned to Hollybrook as the detached and determined diva who stopped at nothing to build a successful business. Could she ever change the way others saw her? She put a hand over her heart.

Through teary eyes, Alexis reread the verse. No, she was too far gone for this. Wasn't she? Or was God speaking to her right now?

Afraid of the possibility of rejection, Alexis slammed the Bible shut and slid it back to where she found it.

Lily's deafening bark erupted from the living room, and her nails clipped on the tile floor in the entrance. Must have seen someone walk by. Or another package. With Carla staying there, wedding and Christmas deliveries had almost been a daily occurrence.

"I'm coming, girl." Alexis glared at the Bible, hopped

down from the stool, and joined Lily by the front door. "Let's see what's going on, shall we?"

Alexis opened the door a crack, aware she was still in her robe, and spotted a brown box with a white label sitting to the side of the door. No delivery van was on the quiet street, but several sets of footprints littered her front path. "What have we here?" She bent over and retrieved the small box, shut the door on the chilly morning, and carried the package to the kitchen island.

Lily looked up at her with pleading eyes.

"I don't think this is for you. Sorry, pup. Huh. It's actually for me?" This one had to be the snow globe Alexis special ordered. Not as exquisite as the one that had smashed, but the best she could source locally.

She grabbed a sharp knife from the wooden block on the counter and cut through the tape securing the package. She hesitated. Should she wait for Carla to come home or call David at the station in case it wasn't what she was hoping for?

No. This is ridiculous. I refuse to live in fear.

Alexis unfolded the flaps and pulled out wads of white tissue paper. Her fingers touched something smooth. Round. Cool. Her heart hammered, and she blew out the breath she'd been holding. With both hands inside the box, her gaze flickered for a moment over to her display case. Morning sunlight bounced off those beautiful snow globes that brought her so much joy.

With a deep inhale, she lifted the glass sphere from the box.

❄

"Thanks again for inviting me." Tom buttoned his coat as he stood outside the entrance of the downtown church. "That was a great service. I appreciate you sitting in the back row with me—and leaving early. Hope I didn't cramp your style too much."

Rhys slapped Tom's back. "No problem. I understand you not wanting people to pry. Hollybrook's a tight community. You're supposed to be on vacation, and I'm sure you don't want to be fielding questions on being a famous author."

"Oh no." Carla stared at her phone. "Looks like I've missed some calls from Alexis. That's not like her. She would never interrupt me at church. Let's head to the cars, and I'll give her a quick ring as we walk."

"Yeah, the church crowd will be pouring through those doors any second." Rhys took Carla's hand, and Tom followed them across the full parking lot.

Tom's stomach tightened at the thought of Alexis's calls being urgent. She didn't seem the needy type, so multiple attempts didn't bode well. He listened to Carla's side of the conversation as they hurried to get out of the cold.

"What's wrong, Lex? No. I'm coming home. Be there in five. Lock the doors." Carla's eyes were wide behind her turquoise glasses. "Can you guys follow me back to Alexis's place? She's had another creepy gift."

Tom's mouth went dry. *This is all my fault.*

Apparently, snowy road conditions did not intimidate Canadians, and Tom clung to the armrest of Rhys's SUV as they raced after Carla. They sped through an upscale neighborhood outside the main downtown area, which took them up the side of a small mountain. The roads were almost deserted this Sunday morning, and they only passed one family walking tiny dogs in festive sweaters. Carla pulled into the driveway of a stylish contemporary house, all angles and huge windows.

"Here we are." Rhys parked behind Carla's vehicle, and all three of them rushed to the oversized black front door. Alexis opened it wide and ushered them inside.

"Are you okay?" Carla hugged her sister.

"Yeah." Alexis's face was void of makeup, her hair was tied up in a bun, and she wore workout clothes. She still looked like a million dollars. "Freaked me out though. Come on in." She peered past Rhys and caught Tom gaping at her. "You're going to want to see this."

They left boots and coats in the spacious entry and followed Alexis into a modern white kitchen with gleaming appliances. Tom's gaze gravitated across the room to the most phenomenal collection of snow globes he'd ever seen. At least twenty-five of them were meticulously displayed in a lit shelved area recessed into the far wall. "Wow."

"My snow globe obsession." Alexis shrugged. "I did warn you I had a thing for them."

Carla peered inside a small brown box on the kitchen counter. "Is this... it? I'm almost scared to look."

"Yep." Alexis used the tissue paper to lift the snow globe from the box and set it on the counter. "Meet the latest in my collection."

Rhys, Carla, and Tom all bent down to study the globe. Whoever was creating these homemade versions was talented. The detail was impeccable. A tiny bookstore. Tom squinted. A man and woman lay on the snow, presumably dead. The woman had long blonde hair.

Carla gasped, and her hand flew to her mouth. "Lex. Is that supposed to be... you?" She glanced at Tom. "And you?"

Tom shook his head as words lodged in his throat.

"This is sick." Rhys put an arm around Carla. "Have you called the police?"

Alexis nodded. "David's on his way. Which could be awkward after our last conversation." Her eyes turned stormy.

"Oh?" Tom seemed to be the only one oblivious to the context of that conversation. When he saw Alexis with David yesterday, they skated together like two lost lovers.

Carla put a hand on Tom's arm. "David's been infatuated with Alexis since they were kids. He has a hard time believing he's not her knight in shining armor. They had *words* yesterday."

"He's not going to like the fact that none of his snow globe gifts are on my shelves either." Alexis nodded to her display. "I can't tell you how many he's sent over the years. And I always return them. Then he leaves them on my doorstep. He's pigheaded."

"Poor guy." Rhys let the words slip and flinched when Carla nudged his ribs. "But yeah, you'd think he'd take the hint."

The doorbell chimed, and a dog growled from the living room.

Tom craned his neck to see the source. "I forgot you mentioned a dog." An English bulldog carrying a little winter weight waddled past them in the direction of the front door, barking as if on a mission.

"Here we go. Another fun fact: Lily hates David. With a passion." Alexis followed the dog to the entrance.

Carla studied the new snow globe. "Either this is the cruelest joke ever, or I'm super worried about my sister." She blinked up at Tom. "You, too. And what if the bookstore gets shot at again? Old Mr. Wiebe was really shaken last week. I don't know if he could handle anything else happening."

"Mr. Wiebe." This was Tom's chance to do a little digging. "Has he been the owner for long?"

"As long as I've been alive." Carla leaned against the kitchen island. "I believe it was passed down from his father and even his grandfather. The family's one of the oldest in Hollybrook. I'm sure he'd love to tell you all about it, you being an author and all."

"I'd like that." *More than you know...*

"Hello." David walked into the kitchen and nodded.

Alexis stood behind him and restrained Lily, who maintained her un-sunny disposition.

"Hey, girl." Tom crouched down and held out a hand to the pup. "You're a beauty, aren't you?"

Lily sniffed at his hand and stopped growling. Her pink tongue set about licking his palm, and she plopped onto the floor in a typical bulldog sploot.

"I can hang out here with her." Tom looked up at Alexis. "We English stick together."

"Wow. All right then. David, check out the latest delivery." Alexis wrapped her arms around her middle and stood next to the officer while he inspected the snow globe. "What do you think?"

David pulled on gloves and held the object in the air. "Are you the only one who's touched it?"

"Yes. And you already have my prints from yesterday."

"And no note?" He slid the snow globe back inside the box.

"Nothing."

David turned to face Tom. "You received any snow globes by chance? Seems you're in the middle of this."

"No." And he wasn't ready to share his concerns with

David. Not yet. Not until he knew for sure who he could trust.

"What's Lex supposed to do about all this?" Carla wrung her hands. "Is there anything *we* should be doing?"

"I'll take this to be processed, of course, but it could be someone playing a prank. Alexis hasn't been hurt physically. It's not like she hasn't ticked off more than a few people in this town in the past." He lifted his stubbled chin. "My guess is they're trying to make a point."

"Which is?" Alexis's face was red.

David folded his arms. "That's for you to figure out, I guess."

What? Tom stood. "Listen, I don't know how things are done here." Tom looked from David to Alexis. "But this is clearly upsetting for Alexis, and I trust the authorities will take it seriously."

"Of course." David lifted the box, and Lily snarled. "We'll have some extra patrols drive by and keep an eye on things. Let us know if there's anything else you think we should be doing, Mr. Harrington. I'll see myself out."

Tom held on to Lily's collar as the officer walked out, leaving an awkward silence in his wake. Once the front door closed, Tom straightened and released Lily. "I think I may have upset him."

Alexis shook her hair free of whatever was holding it up in a bun. Tom stared, mesmerized as her long tresses cascaded in fluid waves around her face.

Their eyes locked, and she smirked. "Don't let him get to you. I don't."

Tom shoved both hands in his pockets. "I'm worried about your wellbeing. What can I do to help?" He lowered his voice. "I'd really like to talk."

"If anyone's hungry, I could make some lunch here."

Rhys rubbed his hands together. "Or you could all come to our place."

Alexis consulted her phone. "We could, but please tell me you guys didn't forget you have a meeting with the wedding decor woman up at your cabin?"

Carla wrinkled her nose. "Oops. That's why you're our wedding planner." She tugged on Rhys's arm. "We should get going, honey. We can eat at the cabin after the meeting. I have no doubt you can rustle up something incredible for everyone."

"No problem. Want a ride up, Tom?" Rhys looked from Tom to Alexis.

"Wait, Alexis should come with us, too." Carla bit a thumbnail. "I'm not comfortable with her being here alone after that delivery."

"I agree." Tom cast a gaze at Alexis. "Let me stay with you."

Alexis leaned a hip against the island. "I don't need babysitting."

"I don't intend to babysit."

Alexis bit her lip. "Fine. You two go on up and keep that appointment. Tom, can you give me ten minutes or so to get ready, and we'll follow in my truck?"

"Of course. I'm in vacation mode. Take your time."

"Great." Carla hugged Alexis. "I feel better knowing Tom is with you. See you soon."

Alexis waited until the front door closed and then turned to Tom. She stood so their faces were mere inches apart. "It's truth time."

"I know." His fingers found the folded book cover in his pocket. "I'm ready when you are."

"Good. I want answers." She lifted her chin. "And

while we're in my truck on the mountain road, I'll keep driving until I get them."

Attractive *and* assertive. Tom's pulse sped up at the thought of spending time alone with her, even if it meant sharing his story.

CHAPTER TEN

"What aren't you telling me?" Alexis gripped the steering wheel with leather-gloved hands and focused on the road ahead. "I want to know everything."

Tom rested an elbow on the center console and exhaled an exaggerated sigh. "There's not much that makes any sense."

"Try me." She was not in the mood for tiptoeing around the niceties of protecting emotions and feelings. "Starting with why you're in Hollybrook. For real."

Alexis attempted to keep frustration from flowing down to her foot on the accelerator. A fresh snowfall last night provided a good covering on the roads for traction, but ice beneath the surface could mean slippery patches on this lower level.

"It's complicated."

"And we have at least twenty minutes to unravel the complications. You weren't very clear on family when I asked you back in the hospital. Trust me, I'm the least judgmental person you will meet. I'm not bothered about backgrounds and skeletons in closets. I have my own. Tell me yours."

Tom adjusted his shades and stared ahead. "I've never been to Hollybrook before, but I've heard a lot about it."

His words were slow and measured, and Alexis held her tongue as she waited for him to continue.

"From my mother. She visited way back... I guess in 1987. She took a year out of University—she dreamed of being a journalist—and came to Canada on a whim. A friend's family lived in British Columbia, so she flew out and worked here in Hollybrook."

Alexis glanced over. His face held such sadness as he talked of his late mom. But Alexis needed details, even if the words pained him. If he—or they—were in danger, she would do all she could to help the situation. "Do you know where your mother worked?"

"Some restaurant. It closed down years ago. I think it was a diner of some sort. But she remembers the bookstore. I mean, *remembered* the bookstore." He cleared his throat. "It was called Happily Ever After even back then."

"Really?" Alexis checked her rearview mirror. The road was deserted, yet a red truck was riding her bumper. She didn't like anyone getting close. On the road or otherwise. Except maybe this mysterious Englishman.

"Mum loved it here, but she was young and impulsive."

Alexis put her foot on the gas in an attempt to put some distance between her truck and the jerk in the baseball cap behind.

"And she fell in love."

Whoa. "She did?" Didn't see that coming.

Tom peered over at her speedometer. "Everything all right?"

"Fine, thank you." Surely, he wasn't about to tell her how to drive.

"I know you're used to driving in these conditions, but I'd rather not end up in a ditch."

Alexis leaned over the steering wheel. "I'm trying to stay ahead of this punk in the truck behind. How about I'll drive, you talk?"

Tom checked over his shoulder. "The red truck? Looks like he's holding back now. I think you may have intimidated him." She could tell he was grinning.

"Good. So, who did your mother fall in love with?"

Tom pulled off his hat and ran his fingers through his hair. "I only found this out when she got really sick. A couple of years ago. She'd carried so many secrets, and it was as if she didn't have the strength to carry them any longer. She was ashamed."

Secrets and shame. Relatable. Another stretch of silence as they continued up the mountain. Several vehicles passed them coming down into town, but the red truck was still on her tail. An uneasiness weighed on her shoulders as she held the steering wheel in a vice grip. Should she be worried? With all the other shady stuff happening...

"Thing is, the man she fell in love with was married. Had a family."

Alexis looked straight ahead. "Messy happens."

"Yeah. Not as much back then. Especially when it results in a baby."

"She got pregnant?" Alexis did the math. Tom could be that baby. He must be about her age, maybe a little older. "What did she do?"

"Mum didn't know she was pregnant until she got back to England. Granny was the one who guessed. Mum dropped out of University, moved back home with Granny, and I came along the following spring."

"Wow." She tried to concentrate on Tom's words, but the truck in the rearview mirror caused her pulse to quicken. Something was not right.

"Yeah. Life was hard for Mum, I know that much. She had to work full-time and never followed her journalism dream."

"But she got to see you become a successful author." Alexis tried to ignore the guy behind and reached over to squeeze Tom's hand. "She must have been so proud."

"She was. I feel like I did it for us both." Tom twisted around. "That truck's awfully close again. Is driving like that normal on this road? Seems risky."

"Where's a cop car when you need one?" She sighed and attempted nonchalance so as not to worry Tom while he was baring his soul, but her gut told her they had a real problem. "I've got it. Sorry. You were saying..."

"I suppose all that to say, I'm trying to find some answers."

"You mean your father? You think he could still be here in Hollybrook?"

Tom turned down the temperature on his heated seat. "No. Mum never got back in touch with him, but she did find out he died. It was a horrific story. He and his family were in a plane crash on their way up North some years ago."

"I'm so sorry. That had to be difficult for you to hear." The accident sounded familiar. "Wait, I remember it happening. The whole community was devastated. But that was the Wiebe family. Old Mr. Wiebe's son and his wife and kid." She tapped her fingers on the steering wheel.

"So... are you telling me Mr. Wiebe at the bookstore is your paternal—"

"Grandfather. Yes, I believe he is. And I have something for him. From my mother." His shoulders relaxed back into his seat. "I have to admit, that feels rather good to get off my chest."

Alexis racked her brain, trying to remember any tidbits about Mr. Wiebe's family. She wasn't aware of any other living family members. He was wealthy. Pillar of the community. And, of course, the kindest man she knew. A friend. No wonder Tom was so sweet. He had inherited that attribute from the bookstore man.

"Thanks for sharing. It's a lot to digest. But I still don't understand why someone would shoot you, particularly if no one knows your connection with the bookstore or Hollybrook."

Tom squirmed. "Well, there is more. Not that I understand why someone wants to hurt me."

"Or me?" Had Alexis unwittingly entangled herself in something bigger when she bought the bookstore? She bit her lower lip. The purchase of Happily Ever After was something she would need to tell Tom at some point. Not yet.

Tom swiveled to face her as she drove. "I promise I have no clue why you're being sent the snow globes. I hope to goodness it's something completely unrelated."

"Unrelated to what exactly?" This was getting more stressful by the minute. The secrets. The snow globes. The story. And her nerves were on edge with the buffoon in the truck behind—

A sudden jolt caused Alexis's head to snap back. She sucked in a sharp breath.

Tom grasped the armrests. "What the heck?"

"That idiot. I can't believe he hit us." Alexis's voice quivered. "I'll pull over as soon as I can. The road widens a bit farther—"

The second impact sent her truck sideways, and a scream filled Alexis's ears. It was her own. A flash of red to her left. Tom yelled. She pulled hard right on the steering wheel and plowed the vehicle into a snowbank at the side of the road.

Silence.

Alexis forced a breath to come and then another. What on earth?

"A-Alexis, are you okay?" Tom's sunglasses had flown off, and his eyes were wide.

She still gripped the steering wheel. "Yes. You?"

"I think so."

"That truck clipped me and sent us flying." Her heart raced, but she needed to be present. "There was no number plate on the front; I checked as we were driving. Did you see anything when he passed?"

Tom shook his head and picked up his shades from the floor. "No, it was a blur. I was sure we were going to end up down the side of the mountain."

Alexis stared at the road before them where the snowbank recessed. "Another thirty seconds, and we would have been." For a stretch, she saw no barrier and every opportunity to leave the road if nudged. "I guess Someone's looking out for you."

"He's looking out for us both." Tom ran a hand down his face. "Whoever was in the truck, they've gone. What now?"

"Let's keep going. Give me a minute." A shudder ran up her spine. "Maybe I'll get some water first. I have bottles in the back." Her hands trembled in her lap.

"I'll get them. I'll check the back of your truck, too. You

stay." Tom lifted her chin and gazed at her with those brilliant green eyes. "You were amazing there, Alexis. Seriously. Thank you."

"An ice queen knows how to keep her cool." She tried to smile, but her chin quivered. She wiped at her wet cheeks. "I'm fine."

"Come here." Tom opened his arms, and she rested her head against his broad chest and staved off more tears that threatened to soak his coat. Bergamot. Cedar. Safe. Warm. He stroked her hair and whispered the sweetest soothing words. Oh, if only she could stay there forever.

But she couldn't. And after that close call with a deranged truck driver, she needed her glass facade back in place. Back into her orb of protection. If she couldn't protect herself physically, she would protect her heart.

"Why don't you let me drive the rest of the way?" Tom's voice oozed concern.

Alexis settled back into her seat. "Thanks, but I can do it. Back on the horse and all that."

"At least let me call this in to the police. Surely, Officer Baxter will want to know."

"I can't take the chance David might answer the call. I can't deal with him right now."

He pulled out his phone. "I can. And after the call, I'll check the back of the truck."

"Then be my guest. I'm sure he thinks I'm overreacting to everything. Which is weird, seeing as how he's the one who's usually paranoid about my safety and well-being. To the point of obsession."

"Let me get you that water first." Tom reached between them to the back seat, retrieved two water bottles, and gave one to Alexis. "Can I ask you something?"

"Shoot." Alexis pulled the cap from her water bottle and chugged half of it.

"How much do you trust Officer Baxter?"

Alexis pondered the question. "Honestly? I trust him with my life."

❄

Alexis waved at Carla, who stood at the blue door of her cabin, chewing her thumbnail and shifting from one foot to another. Alexis leaned into Tom as he put an arm around her, and they trudged from the truck up the snowy pathway. Usually, she would shrug off any attempt that implied she was needy. This minute, she didn't have the energy to argue.

"We're fine, sis. Really." Alexis mashed her lips together.

She might burst into tears at any moment, and she was supposed to keep this bride-to-be calm and happy this week. Carla didn't need the added drama of snow globes and Tom's family mystery. On the drive up, she and Tom agreed not to share his "family news" with anyone yet. So much was going on right now.

"You guys, what happened? Did you call the police?" Carla squeezed Alexis in a hug and pulled her inside.

Rhys came to the door and took their coats. "Is there much damage to the truck? I know a guy."

"We put a call in to the station. And surprisingly, there's very little damage to the truck." Tom shook his head. "I presume that's one of the perks of driving a humongous vehicle around."

"Alexis spends a fortune on gas." Carla closed the door behind them. "But at least she's safe."

"Exactly." Alexis deposited her boots on the rubber mat, gathered her emotions, and stood tall. "I could murder a drink. I guess I'll have to make do with tea. I know you don't have anything stronger here." Rhys told Tom his story of being a recovering alcoholic last night, so it was no secret. Enough secrets were being hidden these days…

"I'll put the kettle on." Carla led Alexis to one of the leather loveseats and covered her with a fur throw. "Sit. Relax. You've had a nightmare of a day."

Alexis shuddered. "I'd rather not talk about it."

Tom hovered at the entrance. "Perhaps I should go. Let you get some rest."

"Come and sit." Alexis patted the space next to her. "At least warm up and allow Rhys to feed you." She glanced at her future brother-in-law. "Feeding people is his love language."

"True." Rhys steered Tom toward the loveseat. "I was in the middle of heating up some of my butternut squash soup. There's a sourdough loaf I made yesterday, too."

Tom rubbed his hands together. "Sounds great. My idea of soup is a can of tomato. Thanks very much."

"Hey, Carla," Alexis called from her spot by the fire. "How did the meeting with the wedding décor woman go?"

Carla bustled back into the living room, bringing with her the aroma of creamy wholesome goodness. "She was super quick. You picked the perfect woman for the job. She's already been here once, so this was a final look-through."

"Is the wedding going to be in here?" Tom surveyed the living area. "It's lovely."

"Thanks." Carla folded her arms. "I adore this cabin. Alexis is the one who did the complete reno while I was working in Mexico; it's all her."

Alexis held up one hand. "I didn't do the actual reno, to be clear. I coordinated everything and made the magic happen. Turned out like a charm. And even though I originally did it for resale, I'm glad you guys are staying here."

"Me, too." Carla looked back at the kitchen where Rhys was whistling as he made lunch. "God's been so kind. And we have some exciting plans for the property."

"But first, the wedding." Alexis tucked her feet under her. "And in answer to your question, Tom, the ceremony is going to be outside under a gazebo my carpenter is delivering on Thursday. Twinkly lights, holly, red ribbon, it's going to be perfect."

"And short." Carla chuckled. "Really, really short. We don't want our guests to freeze. Although we have a blanket for each chair, and they all know to dress warmly."

Tom leaned forward and set his elbows on his knees. "So, after the short-and-sweet ceremony, you and Rhys will have your first dance on the ice?"

"Exactly." Carla's eyes sparkled behind her glasses. "And then we'll all come inside for amazing food. It's going to be an intimate celebration. Neither of us have big families. Mum and Dad fly in from India on Thursday. Rhys's uncle is coming from Seattle, plus a few close friends."

"Including Madison and Chloe. They fly in tomorrow, right?" Alexis's hands were no longer shaking. The change of focus was working.

"Yes." Carla filled Tom in. "Madison is my old boss and best friend from the orphanage in Mexico where I was working until a few months ago. Chloe is her sister—who was instrumental in Rhys and I meeting up again after five years."

"Sisters do have their uses." Alexis examined her perfect nails.

"I envy you." Tom glanced from Carla to Alexis. "Family is precious."

"Oh, man." Rhys rushed in from the kitchen, phone in hand. "This is turning out to be a heck of a day."

"What now?" Alexis's stomach clenched.

Rhys put an arm around Carla's shoulder as he studied his phone. "I got a text from our pastor. Old Mr. Wiebe had a heart attack after church and is in the hospital. He thought we'd want to know."

Alexis's heart sank. Her head whipped around to see Tom's reaction.

His mouth fell open.

Carla wrung her hands. "No. Mr. Wiebe? He seemed okay on Friday when I saw him. I'll bet the stress of the broken window at the bookstore didn't help. Do we know how bad it is?"

Rhys tapped his phone. "I'll try to find out. You want to head down to the hospital?"

Carla grimaced. "Do you mind? He doesn't have family. We can take bread to eat on the go and have soup later." She turned to Alexis and Tom. "Feel free to grab some food from the kitchen. I'm sorry about this."

"Not at all." Tom stood. "I'll be praying. And I should get back to my cabin."

Alexis grabbed his hand. "Can I come with you?" She didn't feel like driving down that mountain road again quite yet. Or being alone. In fact, the whole being alone thing was getting old.

"Of course." Tom pulled her up.

"And, sis, would you keep us posted about Mr. Wiebe?"

"Sure." Carla looked at Tom. "Are you feeling all right? You've gone awfully pale."

He avoided her gaze and rubbed the back of his neck. "Me? Yes, I'm fine."

Carla glared at Alexis.

Alexis shook her head and gave her the *don't ask questions* big-sister look. She squeezed Tom's hand. "Everything will work out. Mr. Wiebe is a strong man. Comes from a long line of good, strong men."

Please, God. I know I have no right to ask for anything, but let this good, strong man meet his grandfather.

CHAPTER ELEVEN

"I'm sure Mr. Wiebe will recover." Alexis locked the cabin door behind them. "He may be old, but he's feisty. I think that's why I like him so much." She eyed her truck, and her chest tightened. "Let's walk over to your place. I need the fresh air."

"Fine by me." Tom offered his hand, and Alexis raised a brow. He winked. "In case you slip."

"In case *you* slip, more like." Alexis buttoned her wool coat and took his hand. Her emotions were a jumble of infatuation for this Englishman, frustration that she didn't seem to be able to keep her distance, and curiosity to know him better.

Their footsteps matched pace and crunched in unison as they circled the lake and passed the other cabins. All was peaceful. At least on the surface. Alexis surveyed the familiar area as they walked, mindful that someone could be watching her. Or him. Or them.

"Would you tell me about my grandfather?" Tom squeezed her gloved hand. "In case I don't get a chance to see him in person. How well do you know him? Sounds like he's close to Carla."

Poor Tom. He'd come all this way. Surely, Mr. Wiebe would pull through. *God, if You're up there listening, would You please not take the sweet old man quite yet? Let Tom speak with him and get his answers.*

"Alexis?"

"Yes, sure. Well, to be honest, I didn't have much to do with him until I came back here after living in Vancouver for a while. Although I think my parents knew him through church."

"He's a Christian?"

"I would say so. Although I'm the last person to ask that question. Carla would know more. She used to go into the bookstore all the time when we were kids. And then, this year, she found out he was going to need someone to work there part-time for a few months, and he was more than delighted to take her on. She's a bookworm. Always has been."

"You're not?"

Alexis dug her free hand into her pocket. "I enjoy reading when I have time. And don't go getting all big-headed or anything, but WWII fiction is a particular passion of mine."

A chuckle rumbled from his throat. "What a coincidence. Mine, too. See all the things we have in common?"

"Ha. Right."

"So how would you describe Mr. Wiebe? Any little tidbit you can give me?"

If only she'd paid more attention. Listened when the old man wanted to chat for longer, and she was in a hurry to get back to work. "He's always been good to me."

"How so?"

She tucked her chin into the top of her coat. Why hadn't she worn a scarf? "I had a bit of a reputation before I went off to University. From popular to heartbreaker to user to used. In a town this small, people talk. Sometimes, I wonder if that's part of the reason why my parents went back to India as soon as Carla finished high school. The malicious gossip about me."

"Surely not." Tom tilted his head.

Alexis swallowed. "I didn't make life easy for them. I rebelled with a capital R. But then everything imploded in my Vancouver life, so I came back here to try again. I was determined to put my head down and become successful. Dear Mr. Wiebe was one of the few locals who treated me like family. Treated me with... kindness. Yeah, he's full of grace."

"Hmm. Thanks for that."

Alexis thought of all the snow globes she'd purchased through the kind bookstore owner. "He goes the extra mile. And he's never judgmental. Never batted an eye when I would order extravagant snow globes from Europe."

"Does he sell snow globes at Happily Ever After?"

Alexis nodded. "A few random ones are dotted around the store. Honestly, I think he'd be happy to get hold of any quirky object for his customers. He researches and sources the snow globes for me. Says they bring back sweet memories from his own childhood. I think he bought a few for himself."

"I like that." Tom squeezed her hand. "Listen, there's something else I need to tell you. I didn't want to share this while you were driving, but I think you should know."

Alexis's breath hitched. This day was like one of those Russian nesting dolls that broke open to keep revealing more of the same. "What now?"

Tom dug into his pocket and unfolded something. "When I first arrived at the cabin, I found this waiting for me on top of the welcome binder in the kitchen."

"Let me see." Alexis held out her hand, and Tom passed over a book cover. *The Paris Whisperer*. The cover where the woman looked like Alexis's doppelgänger. She turned it over, and two words stared back: SNOW GLOBE.

"You all right?" Tom's voice was soft.

Alexis shoved the cover back into his hand and swallowed down bile. "No. No, I'm not." She stopped and glared up at him. "You didn't think it would be a good idea to, oh, I don't know, tell me earlier about this? Or report it to the police?"

Tom held her gaze. "I apologize. When I believed you were about to get married, I thought I could talk to your sister or wait until after the wedding or hope it would come to nothing."

"You were trying to do the right thing. I get it. I think." She scowled. "But something tells me we're in over our heads here."

He pulled her close and hugged her body to his. "I'll keep you safe."

Alexis savored the sensation of his strong arms around her and gave herself a minute to absorb this new nugget of information. "We'll figure this out."

Someone thought she looked like the woman on the book cover. No big deal. The handmade snow globes? They were disturbing. Although she didn't keep her special orders secret, and chances were good that several people in town knew she collected them. Could her acquisition of the bookstore be the issue? Her head ached.

A dog yapped from inside one of the cabins, and Alexis flinched.

"Hey, you okay?" Tom held her at arm's length. "Sorry to drop that on you. Guess I've made you skittish. I won't let anyone hurt you, you know."

Alexis grabbed Tom's hand and resumed walking. "I know. Yappy dog made me jump, that's all." She scanned the trees around the road. She was freaking herself out. "By the way, my English bulldog seems to have taken a shine to you, and she's picky."

"Lily's a sweetheart. And I like to think you have an affection for *all* things English." Tom tried to hide the smile in his voice but failed.

"Rather presumptuous of you."

"Is it?" Tom winked.

"Yes." Alexis bit the inside of her cheek. She was attracted to him on so many levels, but was this guy as perfect as he seemed? "I want to know your intentions."

He raised both brows.

Alexis's cheeks burned. How did he get her so ruffled? "I mean your intentions with the bookstore. Your grandfather. His money."

They approached the little A-frame rental, and Tom pulled a key from his pocket. "His money?"

"That was tactless of me. Forget it." Alexis had no desire to get involved in a family financial situation. She hadn't considered the possibility before, but what if Tom *was* here for money? She frowned. Happily Ever After was going to be hers very soon, and the businesswoman in her couldn't let a captivating pair of green eyes get in the way.

"Wait." Tom stopped walking and turned to face her. "You don't think I'm here for a family fortune or something ridiculous, do you?"

Alexis stared past him to the frozen lake. Cold as ice. Hard as nails. Money was a driving force in her life; could she blame Tom for claiming what might be due to him with an inheritance?

Tom leaned close so their breath mingled in the mountain air. "I'm not some kind of gold digger. I can assure you, I'm very comfortable, thanks to my success as an author. *The Paris Whisperer* will look after me for years to come. Which is just as well."

"What do you mean?"

A muscle in his cheek twitched. "I'm sure you've heard of writer's block. I'm living out the reality and have been for over a year."

Alexis grimaced. "That sucks."

"You have no idea. Another reason to come to the mountains. Inspiration." Tom slipped a hand from his glove and traced his cool fingers down the side of her face. "Although I think I'm already feeling inspired."

"You are?" Caught up in the moment, Alexis clutched the lapels of his coat and pulled him closer.

The intoxicating musky notes of his aftershave was enough to make her melt. Her heart thrummed, and suddenly, she wasn't cold anymore as he lowered his face and kissed her lips with the most gentle, tender affection she'd ever known. Seconds stretched long and slow until Alexis opened her eyes and exhaled, speechless.

"Yes. Definitely inspired." Tom kissed her forehead and then her lips once more. "How about you?"

Words stuck in Alexis's throat. Yes, she found this man attractive and appealing on a hundred levels, but he was visiting. On vacation. Heading back to jolly old England. She had to protect her heart. "Umm, what were we talking about?"

Tom let out a quick laugh, clearly amused. "Money. But truly, I don't care about my grandfather's financial status. In fact, I was prepared to help out should he be struggling. I know how it is for independent bookstores these days."

"I'm fairly sure he's doing well for himself." She lowered her voice. "He has collections of rare books that Carla says are worth an absolute fortune. He even keeps some at the bookstore. Says readers should be allowed to enjoy them."

Tom's lips curved into a smile. "Sounds like a man after my own heart."

"I'd say it's probably the other way around, you being the grandson..."

"Come on." Tom grabbed her hand and pulled her along the path to the red front door. "I have something you need to see. My mum made me promise I would deliver this item in person to my grandfather."

"Good. I'm freezing out here."

This guy seemed to be on some kind of crazy emotional roller coaster today. Scared for their own safety, anxiety over his grandfather's health, and then their magical first kiss... it was all unnerving and unexpected. Alexis tried to avoid the unnerving and unexpected. Yet here she was. Up for the ride and hanging on for dear life.

❄

"Make yourself comfortable. I'll be back in a sec." Tom shed his coat and boots and took the stairs two at a time up to his bedroom. He stopped at the top, and his heart sank.

What?

The place had been turned over. Ransacked. *Why, God? Why is this happening?* Alexis. She was downstairs alone. He ran back down into the living area.

She was filling the kettle with water. "Everything okay?"

"No." He checked the back doors. They were unlocked. He swung them wide open and stepped outside.

"Tom, what are you doing?"

Other than a family out on the frozen lake playing ice hockey, not a soul was in sight. A shiver ran through his body and not from the rush of cold air.

Alexis came behind him. "What's up?"

"Please, come inside." Tom steered her back in and shut the cold out. "Someone was here. Let me make sure we're alone."

Alexis stood by the wall of windows, phone at the ready. "H-how do you know?"

He checked every closet and door as he spoke. "My bedroom's been trashed. And those French doors at the back were locked when I left this morning. Give me a minute." The cabin was a tiny space to check, but he wasn't taking any chances. He went back upstairs and groaned. What a disaster.

Alexis followed him up and rubbed her throat as she surveyed the carnage. "Is anything missing, do you think?"

He blew out a long breath and sank onto the edge of the bed, the weariness and grief of the past twelve months catching up with him.

"Tom?"

Every ounce of energy was required for him to hold his emotions together. He buried his face in his hands. "This is all such a mess."

"We can clean everything up. I'll even help. And I hate housework."

Tom looked up at the beautiful woman before him. The sun shining through the skylight caught threads of gold in her blonde hair. "Can we be completely honest with each other?"

She lifted a shoulder. "I can try."

He patted a space on the bed next to him, and she lowered herself down.

"Talk. And please don't try to protect me. You know I don't do well with that," she said.

"This is going to sound absurd, and I don't understand it myself, but this past year since Mum died, someone has been following me, I'm sure of it."

"Do you have proof?"

Tom shook his head. "I've caught someone's shadow a time or two but nothing concrete."

Alexis's eyes were wide. "The shooting? Was that the first time you've been hurt?"

Tom focused on the wide plank floor. "A couple of months back, I was in a busy area of town and was shoved from a sidewalk packed with pedestrians into the street. Almost got hit by a car. Luckily, my reflexes were on form that day. Of course, no one saw anything, as per usual. I hoped it was an accident, but now..."

"Why? I mean, why is someone so desperate they would hurt you? Or worse? Do you know?"

Tom stood. "I'm not certain, but I believe they may be after the item I want to show you."

"They didn't steal it?" She scanned the upturned room.

"No. Call me paranoid, but I went to extreme lengths."

Sirens sounded from outside, and Alexis froze. "Did you call the police?"

"No. Did you?"

"Not yet." Alexis ran down the stairs, and Tom followed. No way the authorities could have driven from town that fast anyway.

Alexis opened the door, and a police car screeched into the driveway, lights flashing.

"Stay where you are." Officer Baxter took giant strides to the front door, his hand hovering over his gun.

"David?" Alexis stood at the entrance with her arms crossed over her chest. "This is rather overkill. What are you doing?"

"Alexis, are you hurt?"

"Hurt? No. Why would I be hurt?"

"Step aside." He walked through the doorway and looked straight at Tom. David was not happy. "Stay there. Don't even think of moving."

Tom saw the gun and lifted both palms in the air. "I'm not going anywhere." He turned to Alexis.

Her eyes flashed fire. "He can't come in here like that. How did he know about the break-in so soon?"

Tom frowned. "I have no clue."

"David," Alexis shouted up the stairs. "How did you know about this?"

His bulky frame stood at the top of the staircase. "It's Officer Baxter if you don't mind."

She blew a tendril of hair from her face and huffed. "Whatever. Who phoned this in? It wasn't us."

"The call was anonymous. But after my fellow officer received notification from you that there had been an incident on the mountain road earlier on, I wasn't about to take any chances."

"Excuse me, Officer." Tom attempted to stay cool, calm, and collected, but it was no easy task. "I'm the one who has been violated here. Someone broke in and went through my stuff."

"Anything missing?"

"Not that I've discovered yet."

David grunted. "Don't you find that a little strange?"

"For goodness' sake." Alexis raised her voice. "This is ridiculous. The anonymous *helpful* caller is likely the one who did this."

"It's possible. But come up here, both of you."

Tom allowed Alexis to lead the way up to the bedroom.

David nodded his head toward the bathroom. "Have you been in there yet, Alexis?"

"No, can't say I have, *Officer Baxter*."

"You might want to check out the bathtub."

Tom squinted. Had he even looked in there? Only a cursory glance as he was running around like a headless chicken.

Alexis gasped.

Tom joined her. Inside the bathtub lay a collection of glass jars, identical to the ones used for the dreadful homemade snow globes sent to Alexis. *What on earth?*

Alexis searched Tom's face.

Then hers crumpled. "Tom?"

"I swear, I've never seen this stuff before. The bathtub was empty when I left for church this morning. Whoever came in here must have planted these jars..."

Alexis bit her lower lip and shook her head. "I don't know what to think anymore."

"Please, Alexis..."

David put one meaty hand in the air. "Save it. You can give your report to the officer downstairs, Mr. Harrington." David turned to Alexis. "You've had an eventful day. Let me take you home."

Alexis closed her eyes for a moment and then glared at Tom. "Fine. I'm done here."

CHAPTER TWELVE

"You good?" Carla nudged Alexis as they stood shoulder-to-shoulder at the airport the next morning, waiting for Madison and Chloe to arrive. "You can leave me to occupy the ladies today. After the weekend you just had, nobody would blame you."

Alexis sipped her skinny vanilla latte and allowed the warmth to slide down her throat. "No chance. This is my baby sister's mini bridal shower. I'm kind of relieved you already had the big church one last week. I think I can handle the four of us."

"Wish Mom could have flown in earlier." Carla pouted.

Alexis glanced at her sister. This week was a golden opportunity for Alexis to make up for years of selfishness. She had to be present and give the bride all the attention she deserved. "Mom will be here in plenty of time for the most important day. We'll keep you amused until she arrives."

"True. Oh, look—there's Madison and Chloe."

Much squealing ensued from three of the four ladies as they embraced and then waited for suitcases to arrive.

Alexis tried to plaster a congenial smile on her face, but in truth, her heart ached after the revelation yesterday. One minute, she was kissing Tom Harrington, and the next minute, she saw the awful snow globe jars sitting in his bathtub. Had she been too harsh in presuming the worst? Of course, David reveled in a situation that questioned Tom's integrity. This was getting more dangerous by the day.

After almost opening herself up to Tom, Alexis now felt more alone than ever. Better to guard her heart and stay within the emotional snow globe she'd created for herself.

"It's really kind of you to let us stay at your house." Madison linked an arm through Alexis's. Madison was the only woman other than Carla who could get away with such touchy-feely behavior with her. They met last Christmas and bonded over the most stressful time imaginable when Carla was in crisis. Two years in a row... Alexis was going to start dreading Christmas if this kept up.

"My pleasure." Alexis patted Madison's hand. "I've got lots of room."

Chloe heaved her case from the carousel. "I can't believe I get to join in with all this, too. Thanks so much for inviting me." Her immaculate appearance and perfect figure betrayed the fact that she had two little ones at home in Seattle.

Carla gave Chloe a side hug. "If it wasn't for you, Rhys and I might not have met up again."

"God may have had something to do with it, too." Madison spotted her red suitcase and claimed it. "But I'm always grateful to spend time with my favorite sister."

"Your only sister." Chloe looked at Alexis. "You know how it is when they live far away. You have to make the most of every opportunity."

"I do." Alexis had missed Carla during her five years at the Mexican orphanage and was thankful to have her back in Hollybrook again, settling down and living out her dream.

Carla took Chloe's hand baggage from her. "I'm glad you could get away."

"My husband's amazing. And he's about to find out exactly how exhausting it is to wrangle two little ones for a few days." Chloe smoothed her chic blonde bob. "I'm ready for some relaxation."

"Me, too." Madison chuckled. "We're up to fourteen kids at the orphanage at the moment. It's a lot."

"Well, I'm super grateful you both came. Flying back home on Christmas Day was a big ask, and your husbands are the best. We can definitely manage some relaxing girl time. Thanks to Alexis, there's not much left to do for the wedding." Carla beamed. "She's a superstar."

Alexis brushed off the compliment and led the way to her truck as the others chatted about kids and Christmas. Could she even do "relaxing girl time" knowing someone was out there sending harrowing messages…

Or worse?

❄

"This. Is. Perfection." Alexis let out a sigh, which was echoed by the other three ladies in the hot tub.

The day had been delightful and void of any danger whatsoever. Carla took great pleasure in opening a stack of gorgeous gifts, and then they ate the best Mexican takeout as a nod to Madison's husband, Luke, who was holding down the fort at the orphanage. Bless his heart.

Now, as they lounged in the hot tub on Alexis's patio,

pulsating bubbles worked into her knotted muscles while she took in the spectacular view of the snow-capped mountains all around. How did she take this for granted? And tonight, with a thousand stars on display, the clear sky was showing off, especially for her guests.

"I could get used to this." Chloe passed a glass of white wine to her sister.

"Anyone need anything?" Alexis wasn't the greatest hostess, but she was making an effort for her sister.

"Today has been so perfect." Carla looked across at Alexis. "Thank you."

Alexis chuckled. "It's not exactly a wild hen party with fifty women to wrangle, but I think this is more your style."

"Absolutely." Carla wrinkled her nose. "The other option sounds horrific."

Madison agreed as she adjusted the impressive topknot of hair piled up on her head. "Do we have anything on the to-do list for the rest of the week? I hope you'll put us to good use. Bridesmaids duties and all that."

Carla de-fogged her glasses. "Well, we have your dress fittings tomorrow. But the wedding's small, and Alexis is so organized, I think you can pretty much take this week as a vacation and run with it. Do some Christmas shopping. Chill. Right, Alexis?"

"What? Umm, yes. Sure." Alexis struggled to focus on the present conversation, let alone remember what needed to be done for the wedding or Christmas.

"Alexis, is anything wrong?" Madison's big brown eyes, so full of care, were almost Alexis's undoing. "You don't seem yourself. And I completely understand if it's wedding stress. Been there."

"Amen." Chloe joined in.

Madison reached over and touched Alexis's hand. "But please, if there's anything we can do to help."

Alexis blinked back tears and didn't trust herself to speak without blubbering. Was this how a person felt with friends who actually cared? She had Carla, but her sister was obligated to care. This was different. For Alexis, there'd been no true friends since middle school.

"Can I tell them?" Carla whispered into her ear.

Alexis nodded. Why not? The jets finished their cycle, and the night air stilled.

"The past few days have been crazy." Carla explained the situation to the others while Alexis listened to her animated description like it was some fictitious tale. It all seemed too bizarre to be real. Except Tom Harrington. He was real, and he'd stirred her heart.

"I'm so sorry." Madison tilted her head. "And for the record, we've known our fair share of scary, but that doesn't make it any easier for you in this moment. Now, I feel bad about gushing over your gorgeous collection of snow globes this afternoon. If I'd known..."

"Don't worry about it." Alexis shook her head. "Whoever's trying to wig me out by sending those stupid homemade versions, they can't take away my affection for the beauties on my shelf. From the memories."

Chloe tapped her chin. "Hey, Madi, didn't Mom have a snow globe she brought out on display every Christmas?"

Madison grinned. "Yeah, I'd forgotten about that. There was a tiny Victorian Christmas village inside. I'd shake that thing and be mesmerized as the snow fell. Sometimes, I'd even wish I could live inside one of those tiny houses." She tucked a stray lock of brown hair behind her ear. "Especially when I was lonely."

Alexis closed her eyes and breathed in the steam that

hovered above the waterline. How many times had she done the exact same thing? Loneliness came in all shapes and sizes.

"I think I'd like to buy a snow globe from Hollybrook to take home for the kids as a souvenir." Chloe swiveled to face Alexis. "Where do you buy yours?"

"Some are from my travels. The rest I special order at Happily Ever After."

Madison stretched her arms above her head. "Is that the bookstore where you've been working, Carla?"

Carla nodded. "Dear Mr. Wiebe is usually happy to order anything from rare books to collectors' items. He's a sweetie, and at the end of the day, he likes to see the joy on his customers' faces when they find their perfect book—or snow globe. And he adores Alexis."

"Thank goodness he seems to be out of the woods after his heart attack." Alexis sighed. "He's a good man. Salt of the earth." *Like Tom.*

Although those jars in Tom's bathtub were troubling. Alexis still hadn't told Carla that Mr. Wiebe was Tom's biological grandfather. The secret wasn't hers to share.

"Talking of good men..." Chloe took a sip of her wine and fixed her gaze on Alexis. "Do you know what you're going to do about this Tom guy?"

Alexis felt too hot. Claustrophobic, even with the open sky above her. "No, I have no idea what to do, actually." She squeezed her sister's hand. "You ladies feel free to stay out here as long as you like. I'm going to head inside and get ready for bed. Sorry to be a party pooper." She stood, and the icy air stung her skin.

"We're fine, sis." Carla stifled a yawn. "It's been a long day, and I don't think we'll be far behind you."

"Yeah, thanks for everything." Madison smiled. "Hang in there, friend."

Friend. Alexis swallowed the unexpected well of emotion that threatened to erupt at any moment. *Why am I so emotional?* She climbed out of the hot tub, grabbed one of the pink-and-white-striped fluffy towels she'd purchased for this week with the girls, and headed inside to warm up and dry off.

On her way past the kitchen island, Alexis picked up her phone and read her messages.

Several generic check-ins from David. She got the distinct impression he was enjoying this stressful situation. Or hoped she'd break down and come crying into his arms.

Another message caught her eye.

Tom: *Meet me in the morning, Alexis? I'm begging you —let me explain everything. Please.*

Alexis walked barefooted over to her snow globes. She dripped splotches of water from her soaked body onto the black-and-white tiled floor, but she didn't care. She selected one globe from the top shelf, far right. Her first. Not the most elaborate and not the most valuable.

She shook it and watched the sparkly snow fill the globe and then gently fall and settle on the princess and prince as they twirled in a magical embrace. The princess had long, blonde hair like her own, and the prince was tall, dark, and handsome.

Her parents surprised her one Christmas, and from the moment she held the cool orb in her nine-year-old hand, she was captivated. She held a dream.

This was her special possession, the one thing she turned to as a child and as a teen when the words of others hurt, when loneliness was her only companion, when small spaces threatened to choke the life out of her.

Carla, like a good Christian girl, always looked to her Bible and prayed for guidance. Alexis, never feeling fully accepted by her parents, church, community, or even God—she shook her snow globe and wished for love. Her very own prince. But she had looked in all the wrong places.

Her heart squeezed, and she set the precious snow globe back in its prized place on the shelf.

For half a minute, she'd considered Tom Harrington might be her prince. Must be the thought of weddings and romance and Christmas and nostalgia. But no, since his arrival, snow globes had been either smashed or horrid. The only Happily Ever After she was going to end up with had four walls and was filled with books.

She stomped up the stairs.

I'll hear Tom out. I suppose it's the least I can do. And maybe I did react a little hastily—it wouldn't be the first time.

She pictured the deep pools of kindness in his emerald eyes.

I want to trust him, but when was the last time I trusted a man?

Alexis flopped onto her bed and stared at the ceiling.

God, if You haven't given up on me, I could do with a little help here.

CHAPTER THIRTEEN

"You have exactly ten minutes." Alexis dropped her faux fur jacket onto the seat at Angel Cakes and folded her arms across her chest. "I have bridesmaids to take for a fitting this afternoon and a perfect wedding to plan. I don't have time for—"

"Me?" Tom looked at her from across the table with those darned gorgeous green eyes. His puppy-dog pleading pose was better than Lily the bulldog's. "I know. I know you're super busy, and I appreciate you meeting me here this morning." He scanned the bustling bakery. "Neutral ground."

"Hi, Alexis, dear." Molly, the owner, appeared and clutched her hands in delight. "Can I get you and your *friend* something to drink?" She was the sweetest grandmotherly figure for everyone in Hollybrook but also a serial matchmaker.

"Hi, Molly. I'll have a coffee. Black. Please." She offered a smile. "And you'll have to ask my *friend* what he would like. This is a very quick meeting."

Molly's cheeks pinked, and she turned to Tom. "For you, love?"

He lowered his gaze. "Same. Thanks very much."

Molly bustled away, and Alexis flicked her hair over one shoulder. She knew she looked good today. She'd taken her time applying her makeup and curling her hair. Wore killer heels in spite of the overnight snowfall. Let him weep.

"Alexis." Tom checked that they weren't being observed by those nearby and then leaned forward. "Will you hear me out? I don't like the way things were left, and I need you to know the truth."

"Truth? That would be refreshing. We seem to have issues with secrets." Alexis glanced at her gold watch and refolded her arms.

"Right. First of all, the situation in my cabin? I promise you, I was as shocked as you were when I saw there'd been a break-in. And the glass jars in my bathtub? I have never seen them before in my life. I swear. I wouldn't have a clue how to make a snow globe. I haven't done a craft since I was eight years old." He let out an exasperated sigh. "Please, believe me. I did not create or send you those other snow globes. I did offer to replace the one you dropped when I was shot. But if I remember correctly, you declined."

"I did." Alexis maintained a deadpan face, which wasn't easy with the hurt written all over his.

"Here are your coffees, my lovelies." Molly slid a blue chunky mug in front of each of them. "Sure I can't tempt you with anything to eat?"

Alexis cupped her hands around the warmth of her mug. "Not today. Thanks, Molly." Alexis waited until they were alone again. "You were about to show me something back at your cabin. Care to elaborate? Or was that as fictitious as your books?" Zinger. She quirked a brow.

Tom winced. "No, I can assure you this is for real. But as it happens, somewhat ironically—the item *is* a book."

"Okay." Alexis blew on the hot coffee and inhaled the rich aroma. "A book. Must be special."

"Very."

She took a sip of the strong brew. "Where's the book now?"

"Here." He patted a leather satchel on the seat beside him. "I'm not chancing another break-in. This book is valuable but also sentimental."

The yeasty scent of Molly's freshly baked bread tantalized Alexis's taste buds as she tried to concentrate on what Tom was saying. She fixed him with a glare over the top of her mug. "Are you going to tell me what this book is and why you've brought it here?"

Tom nodded. "My mum asked me to gift it to Mr. Wiebe. Apparently, she kept tabs on the store over the years and knew it was still in... in the family, I suppose." He shifted in his seat. "I know she didn't ever want to intrude on my biological father's life. She wasn't a homewrecker. But she hoped Mr. Wiebe senior would still be the owner; that's why I had to come as soon as possible."

Alexis almost choked on her drink. If all secrets were being revealed, she should tell him who the *new* owner of Happily Ever After was. But first, she had to hear him out. "Carry on."

"Mum said Mr. Wiebe was a collector of the finest rare books, and this would be a lovely addition. Her contribution." A genuine longing filled his voice, and he took a moment to swig his coffee. "It's important to me that I follow through on Mum's last wishes."

Alexis's heart broke a little. Try as she might to stay

objective, this man's loss was real, and he was here on a genuine mission. "What's the book? Would I know it?"

"Possibly." He lowered his voice. "It's a first edition of *Peter Rabbit* by Beatrix Potter, the English picture book author. Are you familiar?"

A childhood memory popped into Alexis's mind of sitting up at the cabin with her grandma. A warm summer day. Reading on Grandma's lap. Nibbling on watermelon. "*Peter Rabbit*? Yes, Carla and I had some of those books when we were little. You have a first edition?"

Tom grinned. "I'm glad you know the name. Here's where things get juicy. My great-great-grandmother grew up in the Lake District in England and apparently met Beatrix Potter in person back in the day. She was gifted with a signed copy of *Peter Rabbit* from Beatrix herself."

"That's incredible. What a treasure for your family." And the little book must be worth a fair chunk of change.

"I know. Granny kept it in a safe in her old, terraced house her whole life until she moved into the seniors' home. Before Mum died last year, Granny gave the book to me."

"Does she know you have it here?"

"Oh, yes." Tom cringed. "I'm afraid she's been telling her friends in the home everything. How her grandson is taking her book to a special bookstore where all the best rare collections are kept in a faraway land."

Alexis sat back in her seat. "Isn't that rather risky, seeing as how it's such a collectors' item? Could anyone have picked up on the details?"

"My thoughts precisely. I keep asking Granny to keep quiet, but she says they're half-deaf in the home, and they forget what she says most of the time anyway. They all have their stories to tell, and I think she gets a kick out of hers. Beatrix Potter is quite the legend in the UK."

"Granny sounds a hoot." A smile danced on Alexis's lips. *I think I would like Granny.* "I understand why you want to give this book to old Mr. Wiebe, respecting your mother's wishes and everything. What I don't get is why you were shot and why your place was trashed. Is the book really worth that much?"

"Maybe to the right buyer." Tom rubbed his trim beard. "My flat at home has been broken into twice in the past year."

"Seriously?" Alexis frowned. "You might have mentioned that."

"Let me say it's not as bizarre as you may think. Unfortunately, burglary happens more often than you would expect in England. I installed a security system a couple of months ago, and everything's been fine since then."

"Was anything ever stolen?"

"Not that I know of. Turned over, like at the cabin. I made reports with the police, but what could they do?" Tom clasped his hands on top of the table. "I received a few notes, too. Hand-delivered to my flat. And then the book cover when I arrived at the cabin."

"Are you for real?" Alexis massaged her temples. "What did the notes say?"

"Always the same: WATCHING YOU."

A chill snaked up Alexis's spine. "So disturbing. What did the authorities do about that?"

"Not much. The fan mail I receive is not always complimentary. Comes with the territory. And not considered an official threat." Tom blinked. "I don't know who I can trust here. Thought I'd figure it out on my own."

"And how's that going for you so far, detective?"

"Not great." He reached across the table and touched

her hand. "I'm sorry. I'm truly sorry. I don't understand what the connection is between you and me."

Alexis pulled her hand away and jutted her chin.

He blinked. "I mean, with this snow globe thing or whatever. And why someone has it in for you. The book cover, Happily Ever After, I don't get any of it..."

A crash sounded behind Alexis, and she jumped off her seat.

"Sorry, everyone. My bad." The young server blushed as she scrambled to pick up an array of cutlery spewed all over the floor.

Tom stood and helped Alexis back into her seat. "I don't blame you for being on edge."

"I'm so confused. What do you want from me?" Her face heated, half from her overreaction to the fallen cutlery and half from anger at this ridiculous situation she found herself in by no fault of her own.

"I want you to forgive me if that's at all possible." Tom's Adam's apple bobbed. "This has all gone so wrong. Can we try again? Work this out together?"

Alexis sat motionless for several seconds. Her heart longed to try again. Her head rang with alarm bells. But perhaps she needed to listen to her heart for a change.

"Fine. I forgive you." Her voice was barely audible, but Tom's grin proved he had heard every word.

"Thank you. Thank you so much." He placed a protective hand on his satchel. "I have one more request. Will you come with me right now?"

This man was incorrigible. "Come with you where exactly?"

"I contacted Mr. Wiebe."

"How? Is he even home yet?" Alexis slipped her arms into her jacket. She was anxious to visit Mr. Wiebe, too.

Tom drained the rest of his coffee. "He is. I called the bookstore and said I was an author in town and wanted to meet with the owner briefly. The woman I spoke to actually knew who I was, which was fortunate. Jennifer, I think?" His face reddened. "Anyway, Mr. Wiebe is apparently up for visitors and would be delighted to meet with me."

"At his place above the bookstore?" Alexis had visited his home frequently this past year.

"Yes," Tom said with a grimace. "I know the timing's not the best, but we have a lot to discuss."

"And a book to deliver?"

"Exactly. So, will you come with me? I'd like to strike while the iron's hot." Tom shrugged into his wool coat. "Might be less awkward to have you there as a buffer."

Alexis bristled. "I've never been called a buffer before. And to be clear, this is a favor to Mr. Wiebe. Not to you. I don't like being kept in the dark."

"I understand. No more secrets."

Alexis bit the inside of her cheek. She was going to have to confess about buying the bookstore. "Tom…"

He stood and placed some cash on the table. "Shall we?"

Alexis let out a sigh. "I guess so. I'll text Carla and let her know I'll be back in time to pick them all up for the bridesmaids' dress fittings." She tapped a message out on her phone and then pinned him with a decided stare. "Remember, this sweet man has suffered one heart attack. You don't want to give him another."

Tom shouldered his satchel, and his emerald eyes twinkled. "Why, Miss James, do you have a soft spot for dear old Mr. Wiebe?"

Of course, she did. She also had a deepening soft spot for his grandson.

❄

Huge snowflakes fell as if in slow motion, and Tom resisted the urge to stick out his tongue and catch one. He pinched himself to remember he wasn't in some crazy winter wonderland dream in an actual snow globe. Tom was about to meet his paternal grandfather. On his mother's mission. Together with a beautiful, feisty woman.

Despite the frigid temperatures outside, Tom's insides were warm as hot buttered toast as he walked on the snowy sidewalk beside Alexis. Yes, she was attempting to maintain a frosty exterior with her clipped one-word answers to his questions as they made their way to the Happily Ever After bookstore, but she was thawing. He could tell. Of course, she'd been mad about him keeping some things secret from her, but perhaps she was starting to understand his dilemma. She'd forgiven him and agreed to come with him, at least.

"It's a start."

"What?" She snapped her head around to look at him.

"Nothing. I'm... nervous, that's all."

"I trust you have your speech ready."

Tom's stomach knotted. He'd waited years to pursue his biological family. Not out of discontent or desperation—he was curious about them, plain and simple. Even though he'd imagined this meeting happening a hundred times, he wasn't sure what he was going to say.

"Don't you dare upset him." Alexis raised her chin above the chic wool scarf that covered her long, graceful neck.

Several other pedestrians eyed the pair of them in a not-so-subtle manner. Tom had to admit, he and Alexis made a striking couple as they strode down the street together toward the bookstore. He was finally going to step inside the place his mother spoke of with such fondness.

"Has it changed much over the years?"

Alexis dodged a slippery patch on the sidewalk. "Has what changed?"

"Happily Ever After. Only I need you to know I have no plans to swoop in and take over the bookstore or anything. I'm trying to be transparent with you. No more secrets."

She opened her mouth and then closed it.

Tom nudged her arm. "Were you about to ream me out for something?"

Alexis pulled him over to the library steps, out of the way of busy Christmas shoppers. "No. I have something you should know before we go and speak with Mr. Wiebe." She hitched her purse higher on her shoulder. "In case he pulls a 'granny' on us and decides to blurt out my business."

"Now I'm intrigued." Tom folded his arms and waited for her to explain.

"I do have one more secret." Alexis searched the sky, heavy with snow, and let out a breath. "I bought the bookstore."

"What?" Tom's mouth hung open. *Did not expect that.*

"I take possession on January the first. The deal is hush-hush. I only told Carla a few days ago." Her face was a pretty shade of rose pink as she looked him in the eye. "Say something."

Tom shook his head. This woman was full of surprises. "You're serious."

"Deadly."

A laugh erupted from his throat.

Alexis pursed her lips. "Why are you laughing?"

"I'm sorry." He took both her gloved hands in his. "That

was... unexpected. And utterly delightful. You're going to do fantastic things for Happily Ever After, I know it."

"Really?" She shifted under his gaze. "This may get complicated if Mr. Wiebe decides he wants to hand the store on to you."

"Nonsense. I told you, I don't expect anything from him. I don't need anything. The only treasure he could give me is his time and acceptance and maybe some memories of my father."

"Well, that's a relief. Because you know I would have fought you for the store." Alexis gave him a sly wink.

"I wouldn't expect anything less. And congratulations. You'll have to tell me the whole story later. But I'm anxious to go and meet my grandfather." He released one of her hands and held onto the other. "Come on."

They fell into step once again, and Alexis squeezed his fingers. "That's all the secrets revealed now, right?"

"I sincerely hope so. Except I have to tell this particular doozy to poor Mr. Wiebe, of course."

"Remember he's recently come out of hospital."

"I'll be gentle, I promise. I'm trusting God with this. I'll only tell my grandfather what he can handle for now. If he's frail, I can arrange to meet him in a few days instead."

Alexis nodded, satisfied. "Here we are."

Tom stood outside the Happily Ever After bookstore and shuddered as he stared down at the snow-packed ground. *I was shot in this very spot five days ago.* Although no one would know. The glass had been replaced already, thanks to Alexis and her powers of persuasion. Her pet bulldog was perhaps more fitting for her personality than one might suspect.

"Ready?" Alexis's face paled, and she looked a little... vulnerable? Did she feel nervous standing here, too?

"Absolutely." Tom patted his satchel. "I'll follow your lead."

Alexis swiveled and surveyed the street, bit at her scarlet lower lip, and flicked her long blonde locks behind her. "Let's do this."

CHAPTER FOURTEEN

Alexis pushed open the heavy black door, and the silver bells jangled.

Last time I heard that noise, it was followed by a gunshot.

"Alexis." Jennifer, Mr. Wiebe's assistant, appeared at the entrance of the almost empty store.

"Jennifer. How's the boss?" Alexis pulled off her gloves and slid them into her purse.

"He's fine, considering." Jennifer turned to Tom. "You must be Tom Harrington." She looked him up and down. "I've read your books." She sounded underwhelmed.

Tom stomped his boots on the welcome mat. "Umm, thank you. That's... kind." He frowned at Alexis.

She shrugged. Weird that Jennifer wouldn't be gushing over a famous author in their little store. Rude.

"I'm going to finish up with these two customers, and then I can take you to Mr. Wiebe. Please, take a seat or have a look around." Jennifer spun on her heel and sashayed back to the cash register, where an elderly couple clutched several books.

"She's not exactly a ray of sunshine, is she?" Tom's whisper rose above the sound of Christmas carols playing in the background.

"Welcome to Hollybrook." *And I'll be having a word with that girl once I'm in charge.* "Feel free to check the place out." Alexis was interested to see his first impressions.

Tom turned in a circle as he perused the store. "Nice." He nodded. "Cozy ambiance. Looks like the store's well laid out. And I love the cute kids' section. I think that's important, you know? My love of books began at my local bookstore, where I could sit and read while Granny took her time picking out a romance for her or a thriller for Mum." He sauntered to a reading nook with a collection of comfy wingback chairs. "I could spend a lot of time lounging here."

Good to know. Alexis had plans for Happily Ever After. In her travels, she'd taken extensive notes in all her favorite bookstores: what made them unique, welcoming, aesthetically pleasing, and easy to navigate. But she also intended to keep its authentic vibe. The store had to be something old Mr. Wiebe would be proud of, too.

The silver bells jangled, and Alexis pivoted to see Jennifer holding the door open for the customers on their way out. *Maybe she's not all bad.* She then turned the sign on the door to "CLOSED."

"Why are you closing?" Alexis joined her at the entrance. "A little early for a lunch break, isn't it?"

Jennifer's neck splotched with patches of red. "I'm here on my own, in case you hadn't noticed. Your sister is on vacation because of her *wedding,* Sylvia called in sick, and Mr. Wiebe—well, he'd love to come and help, but doctor's orders are that he stays upstairs a few more days."

"Sylvia's sick?" Alexis saw the new mom and her baby

in Angel Cakes having coffee less than an hour ago. Her mouth twitched. She wasn't going to rat her out. Maybe the baby had a rough night.

"Follow me." Jennifer was already heading toward the rear of the store, where the staircase led to Mr. Wiebe's apartment.

Alexis had been here recently signing papers, asking questions, and picking the brains of a lifelong bookseller. She should have brought him something today. Flowers. Chocolates. Oh well, a grandson would have to suffice.

❄

Tom shifted from one foot to another as Jennifer knocked on the apartment door and then pushed it open. His pulse raced as he strained to see the first glimpse of his grandfather. He followed the ladies inside and inhaled the comforting, familiar scents of old books and coffee.

"Hi, Alexis, dear. I presume you've come along with our English author. I heard you two were acquainted."

Alexis walked over to a fireplace where Mr. Wiebe sat in an armchair. His feet were propped up on a small, padded stool, and a sturdy-looking walking cane leaned against a side table.

Tom stood at the open door and gawked. This was his grandpa. He tried to absorb everything at once. A kind face with a dimple on each cheek. Almost-white hair neatly combed off his wrinkled forehead, with a matching mustache and a trimmed goatee. A polka dot bowtie and buttoned-down shirt beneath a cable knit cardigan. And the very best—twinkling bright green eyes the same shade as his own.

"Tom? Come and meet Mr. Jeremiah Wiebe." Alexis

beckoned him in, and he entered the overly warm living room.

Mr. Wiebe started to rise, and Tom put out a hand. "Please, please, don't get up. I know you've not been well. It's awfully good of you to agree to see me."

The old man put out a weathered hand, which Tom shook, savoring the moment their hands connected skin on skin. *This is surreal.*

"Do take a seat, both of you. Make yourselves at home. Would you like some coffee? I'm afraid it's the awful decaf stuff. Doctor's orders."

Tom, rendered mute, slid out of his coat and sank into a loveseat. Alexis did the same and perched next to him.

"No, but thanks. We just had coffee," Alexis answered for them both. "How are you feeling today? You gave us all quite the scare, you know."

Mr. Wiebe stroked his goatee. "A lot of fuss about nothing, really. I'll be good as new in a day or so. They need me down in the bookstore this week. Christmas is our busiest time. Isn't that right, Jennifer? Oh dear, she's gone already."

Tom turned, but Jennifer had indeed disappeared. That girl was a bit of an odd duck.

"She said she was on her own down in the store." Alexis checked her watch. "Do you want me to call Carla? I'm sure she wouldn't mind popping in for a few hours after the bridesmaids try on their dresses."

Mr. Wiebe scratched his head. "Sylvia should be in today."

"Try not to worry. I'll ask Jennifer on our way out." Alexis looked up at Tom. "I know you'd much rather chat with Tom Harrington."

"Yes, yes, of course. Always a pleasure to have an author visit us in person. Tell me about yourself, son."

The term of endearment caused Tom's chest to constrict. *Lord, please show me the gentlest way to share my news.*

"Well, let's see." Tom fidgeted with the clasp of the satchel on his lap. "I think I need to apologize first for the incident with your window last week." He placed a hand on his chest. "It's all rather a mystery, but I'm terribly sorry your bookstore was caught in the crossfire. Literally."

"Our Alexis got the window all fixed up; think nothing of it. I'm glad to see it didn't do any permanent damage to you."

Our Alexis? She really was close to this man. "No, I'm right as rain. A graze and a little bump. But I wanted to visit the bookstore at some point because I have something to give you." Tom unlatched the satchel and retrieved the copy of *Peter Rabbit.* "This is for you."

Mr. Wiebe reached out his hand and accepted the book. "Well, what do we have here?" He pulled a pair of gold wire-rimmed glasses from the side table and slid them onto his nose. A smile curved his thin lips as he turned a page and read the inscription. "A signed copy by Miss Potter herself? And personalized to 'a friend?'" He raised bushy eyebrows. "May I ask where you got this, son? And why you would want to give away such a treasure?"

Alexis squeezed Tom's arm.

"It's rather a long story. But my mother died a year ago—"

"My condolences, dear boy." He removed his glasses.

"Thank you. Before Mum died, she asked me to come here and give it to you in person. It's been a prized possession in our family. My grandmother received this very book from her grandmother, who was gifted it by Beatrix Potter on a visit to the countryside. She was a family friend, apparently."

Mr. Wiebe studied the book with awe and reverence. "Fascinating. Did I know your late mother?"

Tom rubbed his now-sweaty palms on his jeans. "It appears she knew your son."

He looked up. "She knew my Robert?"

Okay, Lord, here I go. "Yes. My mum was here many years ago. 1987. She met your son, and they became friends... and then more than friends...they actually had a... relationship. Intimately." This was beyond awkward.

Alexis hurried over and kneeled next to Mr. Wiebe. She held his hand and gave it a squeeze.

Tom mouthed his thanks to her before continuing.

"Mr. Wiebe, there's no easy way of explaining this, so I'll simply say it. I know your son was already married at that point, and my mum didn't know she was pregnant until she returned to England."

"Pregnant, you say?" Mr. Wiebe's face was pinched, but his eyes were bright as he listened and nodded.

"Yes. She told me she didn't want to hurt anyone. Didn't want to mess up your son's life. So, she gave birth to me, and we lived with my grandmother, and Mum kept tabs on this bookstore all these years. Said visiting the store brought her immense joy during her stay here. It's where she met my... biological father."

"Are you alright?" Alexis rubbed Mr. Wiebe's hand.

He nodded. "I'm a little shocked. But I remember her. Truly, I do. I recall your mother spending hours in Happily Ever After. Her English accent was a novelty in these parts back then. I also remember my dear wife voicing her concerns to me when she saw the way our married son looked at your mother."

"Really?" *Interesting.*

"She was always right, my wife. Didn't miss a thing. I guess they had what you kids call *chemistry*. Your mother was a beauty. And yes, she did love her books." He shook his head. "Well, well, well. So, let me get this straight. Are you telling me I have a grandson?"

"Only if you want one." Tom spread his hands. "I'm not asking for anything."

"No, you're giving." Mr. Wiebe held the book in the air. "I acquired a precious book and a precious grandson. Who'd have thought?" He let out a sound that was half-laugh and half-cry. "God is good. Come here, son."

Tom walked over and gave his grandfather a gentle hug, mindful he was in less than perfect health. "Thank you. I suppose we have lots to talk about."

"And I have all the time in the world." Mr. Wiebe set the book in his lap. "Where shall we begin?"

A crash sounded from below.

Heavy footsteps rushed up the staircase.

The apartment door flew open.

Tom gasped. "Uriah Borne? What are you doing here?"

His former best friend stood in the doorway brandishing a gun. A gun?

"No one move a muscle." Uriah waved the weapon. "I'm not afraid to use it." He looked straight at Tom. "As you now know."

Tom's mind swirled. This didn't make any sense. "You're the one who shot me?"

"What do you think?" Uriah snarled. "That was a nice little warning. Like all the others. It's been a while, Tommy, hasn't it?"

"Could someone explain what is going on here?" Alexis

stood as still as a statue, one hand gripping Mr. Wiebe's shoulder.

"I'm taking what's mine. And a bit extra for my effort. Right, Jen?" Uriah stepped into the room, and Jennifer appeared from behind him carrying a bunch of plastic zip ties.

"Jennifer?" Mr. Wiebe's voice shook. "Whatever are you doing?"

"She's with me." Another snarl from Uriah.

He'd hardened since Tom saw him last. Tom learned Uriah was in trouble financially with gambling or something, but rumor was he'd pulled his life together and was working at Granny's seniors' home. Come to think of it, Granny mentioned his name several times in the past year.

"What's going on?" Alexis sounded mad. Didn't she see the gun?

"Here's the thing, sweetheart." Uriah trained the gun on Tom as he walked toward her. "My writing mate here thinks he's the only one who's in the know with the book world. But I've been watching him. Listening to Granny. Biding my time. And now I've come to collect."

"His granny? Collect what? Books?" Alexis narrowed her eyes.

Uriah grabbed the Beatrix Potter book from Mr. Wiebe's trembling hand and shoved it inside his coat. "I've been listening to the story of how this one came into your family since we were school kids, Tommy. Thing is, my family reckons it belongs to us. Our families go back."

"That's nonsense." Tom shook his head.

"I've had my eye on it for years. Used to be in your granny's little safe. Guess she should've kept it there. She tells me everything, you know."

Tom's dear grandmother had unwittingly shared her

precious information with a criminal. "You've been using my grandmother?" Tom's heart sank. "You better not have hurt her." Although he'd spoken with her yesterday, and she was her usual chipper self.

"Yeah, she's fine. I'm not an animal." He sneered. "Remembered me from the old days. She's super chatty. But I'm not. Let's do this, Jen." He nodded for her to tie up Mr. Wiebe.

"Wait, he just had a heart attack." Tom went to protect his grandfather, and Uriah waved the barrel of the gun inches from Tom's face.

"Timing sucks." Uriah's tattoos rippled on his thick neck.

"I'll be gentle." Jennifer put the old man's hands in a prayer position in his lap and fastened them together with one of the zip ties.

"Jennifer?" The old man's voice was laced with disappointment.

"You're next." She tied Alexis's wrists together with the practiced precision of a seasoned professional and then hurried over to do the same with Tom's. She cinched them nice and tight.

"Old man, you stay put." Uriah cleared his throat. "Give us the code for the safe room, and we'll be out of your way."

"With all my books?" Mr. Wiebe looked from his employee to the thug with the weapon. "How do you two know each other?"

Jennifer set her hands on her wide hips. "We met online."

"Shut up, Jen. That doesn't matter. Let's get in and out. Old man, the code. *Now*."

Tom's stomach clenched as he stood helpless. He'd

dropped a bombshell on Mr. Wiebe, and now his whole world of books was about to implode. What could he do? Uriah always was hotheaded, and Tom couldn't chance anyone being injured or worse. Not his grandfather. Nor Alexis. *God, we need You.*

CHAPTER FIFTEEN

Alexis's chest tightened, her temper ready to explode. She knew Jennifer was up to something. Guilt was written all over her face when they were downstairs. The store was now closed to customers, so they had no chance of being rescued, and this short, stocky dude—the old friend of Tom's—had an actual gun trained on them. The realization that he wasn't hiding his identity from them didn't sit well either...

"What are you going to do with us?" Alexis's voice faltered. "If Mr. Wiebe gives you the code, how do we know you'll let us go?" The code could be their one and only bargaining chip.

"That's a chance you'll have to take. You scared to die, sweetheart?" The obnoxious man leered.

Was she? Did she know for sure where she'd be going? What would everything she lived for until now matter if her life ended today? Her plan was to pour into the community with the purchase of the bookstore, leave a legacy of some sort, make a difference, and find acceptance—but she hadn't been given the opportunity yet. And this punk wasn't going to snuff out her light.

She bit the inside of her cheek until she tasted blood. "No, I'm not scared."

"Uriah, what are you thinking, man?" Tom held up his bound wrists. "If you want money, I've got money. Tell me how much, and I'll wire it to you."

Uriah laughed, the sound menacing. "That would be way too painless for you, my old friend. This plan has been in the works for a very long time. Ever since you left me in the dust and became rich and famous. Book buyers are chomping at the bit. The black market is very excited about all these rare and sought-after editions. Jen and I will soon be living in the lap of luxury where no one will find us."

Jen clung to one of the bald guy's biceps and smirked like she'd won the crown jewels. What possessed this regular bookworm to get involved with such a despicable human?

"Old man. Give me the code, or your author friend here will get a bullet in his writing hand." Uriah aimed the gun ready. A muscle popped in Tom's jaw.

"Fine, fine. Please, don't hurt anyone." Mr. Wiebe raised watery eyes to Jennifer. "The code is 12–24-60. Right, left, right."

12-24-60. Alexis memorized the numbers. Christmas Eve, 1960. That was Mr. Wiebe's wedding day. He'd told her so when Carla and Rhys announced they were getting married on Christmas Eve.

"Go." Uriah nodded at Jennifer, and she scurried through the living area to Mr. Wiebe's bedroom.

Of course, Jennifer knew about the room with the walk-in safe containing the prized rare book collections. She'd worked here forever as a trusted member of staff. Alexis only knew the room existed because Mr. Wiebe showed her around when she bought the bookstore. The apartment would remain his, but he wanted her to know about the special room.

"You two, follow her." Uriah gestured with his gun, and Tom walked behind Alexis as they filed behind Jennifer and left Mr. Wiebe with the gunman. "Don't try anything funny—I've got the old man here, remember."

Alexis's stomach churned as she entered the bedroom. The space still held hints of Mr. Wiebe's late wife with its cabbage rose floral quilt over the king-size bed and lace curtains at the window overlooking Main Street. No wonder he chose to stay here as long as possible with all his memories. But what now? And what was the matter with Jennifer? She'd worked at Happily Ever After since high school. Steady-Eddy type. Maybe Alexis could appeal to her sense of decency.

"Hey, Jennifer." Alexis kept her voice low as the other woman worked on the safe combination on the door. "Is that guy threatening you? Do you need help? Surely you aren't going to up and leave Hollybrook? Your family? Your sister, Jane?"

Jennifer pivoted, her face inches from Alexis's. "Are you kidding me? I've been stuck in this hole my entire life. This is my escape. Uri loves me. We've been planning this for months. And you, ice-queen lady, are not going to stop us. Wait here and shut up." With that, Jennifer pushed the thick door open and walked inside the tiny room.

Alexis looked up at Tom. "What are we going to do?" Her voice was a whisper. "They're not going to let us go now that we can identify them."

"I think I can distract Uriah," Tom spoke into her ear.

"If you can trap Jennifer." He nodded at the room where Jennifer was gathering a series of boxes.

"Okay." Only one way of doing this. She gritted her teeth. "Lock us both in there."

His eyes widened. "You sure?"

Alexis took a deep breath. "No. Just do it." She reached up and kissed him hard on the lips, drawing strength she knew she would need. "Make sure you come back for me."

❄

Tom didn't have time to think. He pulled the heavy door shut behind Alexis and twirled the dial around and around, shutting her into a small space he knew would be her undoing. *Lord, please help her.*

He needed to resurrect his limited high school performance acting experience and make this next part convincing.

"What's taking so long?" Uriah's voice boomed from the living room.

"Uriah." Tom stumbled from the bedroom, panting as both men stared at him wide-eyed. "You better get in there, man. Something's happened to Jennifer. I don't know what's wrong with her."

Uriah shoved Tom to one side and stomped into the bedroom. "What the heck?"

Tom stared into his grandfather's fear-filled face and pulled him up out of the armchair with his bound hands. *"Go now. Get help."*

Uriah growled and turned back to Tom. "What have you done?" He'd seen the closed safe room. "And where's the old man going?"

Tom grabbed the walking cane and lunged at Uriah's torso with all his might.

The apartment door slammed.

Gunshot.

Silence.

CHAPTER SIXTEEN

The thick door slammed, and Jennifer gasped. "What are you doing?"

Alexis took a steadying breath. Two women. Her own wrists were bound. No weapons. She scoured the shelves. The tiny, windowless room. Like a padded cell. Panic built in her chest. *Not now, God. Please.*

"Uriah's going to kill you for this, you know." Jennifer's face was as red as her splotchy neck. She bared her teeth. "Or that Tom Harrington. He deserves to die."

"Why would you say that?" Alexis spotted a row of snow globes to her right. Big ones. Dear old Mr. Wiebe had his own collection.

Jennifer banged on the heavy door. "Didn't you know? Tom and Uriah were supposed to be best friends. Do everything together. Co-authors even. But Tom dropped him as soon as the going got tough."

"Looking at that bozo, I can imagine the stuff he was into."

Jennifer stood in front of Alexis so they were eye to eye and slapped her cheek with an open hand.

Alexis's skin stung. She could feel her pulse race, and she desperately needed air, but she couldn't show weakness. "Tom can't help being brilliant and successful."

"You think you're better than everyone else in this town when you have the worst reputation. Prancing around with your stupid snow globes that cost a month of my salary. I've seen the special orders." Jennifer sneered. "Who do you think created your homemade snow globe gifts?"

Jennifer had been busy.

Alexis couldn't breathe in this room. *Focus on Jennifer.* "Why? Why are you doing this and involving me?"

"It was perfect. When Uri approached me, I researched Tom Harrington and his lame books. Saw that cover with the woman who could be your twin. The plan was put into motion."

"How long have you been scheming?"

"Long enough to get to know you both. To know your plans to buy this place. Who do you think you are?"

A muffled gunshot sounded from outside. Both women flinched.

Jennifer pounded the door. "Uriah?"

"Who do I think I am? You seem to think I'm an ice queen." Alexis reached up and grabbed the nearest snow globe in her bound hands and smashed it on the back of Jennifer's head with all her might.

The snow globe exploded, showering the area between them with glitter and liquid and particles of faux snow.

Jennifer steadied herself with one hand on the door before slumping to the floor, surrounded by shards of glass. She didn't move.

A stale silence filled the air. Alexis froze to the spot. *What have I done?* And who had been shot out there? Tom? Her heart squeezed. Deep breaths. She was in a wretched small room with tied wrists and an unconscious woman on the floor. *Please, don't let her be dead.* She crouched down and touched Jennifer's wrist. A solid pulse. And way more regulated than her own. Hot. So hot in here. If she could only breathe...

Palpitations hammered in her chest. Focus. She needed to focus on one thing for a few seconds, get her mind back in the game. She turned to the row of snow globes and picked one up. The scene was of a Christmas tree surrounded by wrapped gifts. She shook the orb and watched the snow dance and float, suspended in liquid. How many times had she done this very thing to calm her nerves over the years? She honed in on the Christmas gifts and reminisced on Christmas Eves from her childhood, so full of joy and hope.

Breathe. Jesus had been the Greatest Gift back then. She knew that deep down. Somehow, along the way, she was distracted by the shiny things in life. Boys and popularity, then money and success. Was it too late for her to be accepted? *Breathe.* Not only by Hollybrook but by God?

For a brief moment, Alexis was calm. Like a fresh covering of snow had fallen over her, leaving the gift of peace. Perhaps too much peace. No noise came from beyond the thick door. And she had no clue whether Tom or Uriah would be opening the door next. Either way, she had to get out of here somehow.

"Jen?" Uriah's muffled voice made Alexis squirm in her own skin.

No. Did this mean Tom was injured—or worse? Tears trailed down her face as she slid down the wall next to the door. Surely not. Somehow, this handsome man with the English accent and the emerald eyes had broken into her life, smashed through the snow globe of her own making, and captured her heart. The way he spoke about God, his mom, his granny, and his writing. He was one of a kind.

"Jen, what the heck is going on?" Thuds on the door.

Alexis shut her eyes tight and concentrated on breathing. Was this actually happening? If only she hadn't left her phone in her purse. If only she could think clearly, beyond these four walls that were closing in on her by the minute. If only she knew Tom was safe. Alive.

God, I know You see me in here, even if no one else can.

"Jen? Answer me."

Alexis blinked and stared at Jennifer's limp body on the floor next to her. What was this girl thinking? Trying to steal from a kind old man and run away with a criminal? More books were stacked in here than Alexis imagined. Her suspicions were probably spot on; old Mr. Wiebe's stellar collection was worth a fortune. One book lay open at the end of the shelf. That particular book hadn't piqued Jennifer's interest, but it must be dear to Mr. Wiebe.

"Jen. Jen."

The trembling in Alexis's body lessened, and she stood to inspect the book. A Bible. And the wise old man had underlined a section from Psalm 139:

"God, investigate my life;
get all the facts firsthand.
I'm an open book to you;
even from a distance, you know what I'm thinking.
You know when I leave and when I get back;
I'm never out of your sight."

Alexis blocked out the sounds from beyond the door and let the words wash over her. She was never out of God's sight. Even when she balked and rebelled and thought she could do better without Him, He saw her. Knew her like no one else did. The good, the bad, and the horribly ugly. This open book said *she* was an open book to God. And still, He loved her.

Father, that's all I ever wanted, isn't it? To love and to be loved? To have my happily ever after... not by investing in a bookstore or making a difference in my community or even finding a man to spend my life with. My happily ever after—it can only be found in You.

Another tear slid down her cheek and splashed onto her bound hands. "I don't want to be bound anymore." She crouched to the floor and selected a shard of glass. Careful not to cut herself in the process, she set about breaking the zip tie as she prayed that whatever was happening outside the cocoon of this safe room, somehow Tom would be alive and well and ready to hear how God was thawing her frozen heart.

CHAPTER SEVENTEEN

Tom stilled on the bedroom floor and played dead. His right shoulder had taken a bullet this time, preventing him from going for help. He'd have to leave that to his grandfather. He covered the wound with his tied hands, and the warm ooze of blood spread through his fingers. *Must not pass out.* He'd stuck Uriah like a pig with the end of the cane, and his stomach had to be hurting him. Still, Tom hadn't been fast enough to stop that trigger-happy finger.

The injury he inflicted upon Uriah knocked the wind out of the shorter man for the moment, at least. In those seconds of silence, Tom staggered over behind the massive bed and was able to take stock and stay out of sight. But the silence was short lived. Now, while Tom lay still, Uriah pounded on that door, intent on getting the valuable books and Jennifer. Mostly the books, if he knew Uriah.

"Jen." More banging on the door.

Tom's shoulder was on fire as he fumbled around for the cane. He'd dropped it in the scuffle, and his grandfather's stick was the only weapon Tom had at his disposal. The elderly man had escaped; that was something. *Please, God, keep my grandfather safe and let him find help for us. And don't let Uriah think him worth pursuing.*

As long as Alexis was in that room, Uriah couldn't hurt her—unless Jennifer remembered the code and shouted it out. The door was thick, but why was no sound coming from either of the ladies? *Father, be with Alexis and give her Your peace...*

Tom patted beneath the bed and winced as the pain sliced through him again. A little farther, and he touched the smooth wood of the cane. And the heavy, ornate, bulbous shape on the top. He'd used the small end last time, but if he could surprise Uriah from behind with the weight...

"Jen. Answer me."

Tom recognized the rage in his old friend's voice. That unfettered anger had taken him on a slippery slope as a youth. Uriah was smart. A good writer with potential. But when he lost his temper, he made poor choices. And if he did manage to get inside the safe room, Alexis would take the brunt of his rage. That couldn't happen. Two things Tom had in his favor were his height—and his God.

Father, I need a surge of strength. Enough to take this madman down. And keep Alexis safe.

Tom filled his lungs with air, grabbed the middle of the stick, blocked out the pain, and in one smooth motion stood, lunged across the end of the bed, and brought the silver sphere on the end of the cane down on the top of Uriah's shaved head.

The sickening thud of metal on bone filled the room.

Uriah dropped the gun to the carpet, fell to his knees, and keeled over to one side, out cold.

Tom remembered to breathe as he stood with the cane

in his hands, still tied together at the wrists. His shoulder smarted, his own knees buckled, and he kicked the gun to the entrance of the bedroom as he leaned heavily against the safe room door. Flickers of light like tiny stars marred his vision. He blinked them away. *Must stay awake.*

"Alexis? Alexis, it's me. Tom." He didn't have the strength to bang on the door.

"Tom?" Her voice was faint, like cotton was stuffed in his ears.

He glared down at Uriah. He wasn't going anywhere, but Tom needed medical assistance soon, and Alexis could be having a panic attack in there—or she could be injured. This Jennifer was a wild card.

"I want to get you out. You're going to be okay." He dropped the cane and pressed his fists against his shoulder. "The number. What was the number for the safe? I remember the last two digits were *sixty*." *Please tell me you know this.*

Silence. Seconds stretched.

"I remember. You ready?"

"Yeah. Yell them out." Tom rested his sweating forehead on the wall above the dial. "Go."

"12–24-60."

He repeated the numbers.

"Yes. Right, left, right."

"Got it." Tom cupped his trembling hands together and concentrated with every ounce of energy he could muster as he turned the safe dial.

A satisfying click. The door opened, and he stumbled into Alexis's arms.

"Tom." She helped him over to the bed and gasped when she spotted Uriah's body on the carpet. "And you've been shot?" She balled up some bedding, which she pressed against his shoulder.

"Again." He winced as his adrenaline slowed and pain took over. "We have to stop meeting like this. You're okay?"

"I am now." Alexis kissed his lips, this time soft and tender. Come to think of it, her whole countenance appeared soft and tender. Calm. Serene.

She glanced up at the bedroom window. "I see lights outside. Police must be here already. How?"

"Old Mr. Wiebe." His words slurred. "Grand-p-a."

"Thank goodness he's safe."

"Where's Jenn.... Jennifer?"

"I hit her with a snow globe." Alexis kissed his forehead. "And, Tom, I have so much to tell you..."

"Wait. What?" The flickers of light returned to his vision, only now they looked like the mesmerizing particles of snow in a snow globe...

❄

"This is so déjà vu." Alexis settled into the plastic chair beside Tom's hospital bed. His eyelids looked heavy, and his hair was disheveled and giving off those attractive first-thing-in-the-morning vibes. "How do you feel?"

Tom exhaled, and a relaxed smile crossed his face. "Better now that you're here. And now that my shoulder's been fixed up. Did you get yourself checked?"

Alexis rubbed her indented wrists where the zip ties made their mark. "I'm fine. No harm done. And your grandfather had the all-clear to leave, so Carla drove him back to my house to rest. Madison and Chloe are on caregiving duty with him while Carla cleans up his apartment and checks on the bookstore."

"Happily Ever After is still open after all the drama?"

"Apparently." Alexis crossed her legs. "Sylvia's helping out. All hands on deck. I don't know why they didn't close for the day, but I'm guessing this will be good for business with all the looky-loos coming in to get the latest gossip."

"Ah, the gossip. Are you ready for it?"

Alexis ran her fingertips over the fresh marks on his wrists. "I am actually. We all survived, and I happen to believe Someone was watching over us."

Tom tucked a wayward strand of her hair behind her ear. "For sure. Granny must have been praying again."

"I'd like to meet your granny one day."

Tom chuckled. "You two would be thick as thieves. Talking of whom, do we know what happened to Uriah and Jennifer?"

Alexis chewed the inside of her cheek. "Yeah, they're here in the hospital. David made sure there are police officers outside both rooms. They're going to be questioned as soon as they get permission from the doctors, and then they'll be taken to jail until trial. I know they both have issues and need help—but I hope they get what they deserve... it could have ended so much worse. Any one of us could have been killed."

Tom reached over and clutched her hand. "We need to trust the authorities, including Officer Baxter. I feel like he's been blinded by his jealousy up until now."

"He'll get over it." Alexis studied Tom's face. "He'll have to get over me."

"Yeah?" Tom's mouth twitched. "Why's that, Miss James?"

Her warm heart soothed her insides like a hot cup of cocoa. "Seems I'm smitten by this dapper English author who insists on melting my frosty exterior." Although, what would this look like going forward? She frowned. He lived in England, and she had purchased the bookstore here in Hollybrook. Then there was Carla and old Mr. Wiebe...

"Hey." He reached over and squeezed her hand. "Penny for your thoughts?"

"I don't think even you could afford all the stuff jostling around in my brain." Alexis stood as she let out a long sigh and peered down into his eyes, as green as the pine trees outside. "I told you about my moment I had with God in the safe room. I know He sees me and knows me and loves me... problem is, I don't like not being in control. I want to know what's going to happen. With Uriah and Jennifer. With giving up my realtor life. With Happily Ever After..."

"And our happily ever after?" Tom pulled her down toward him with more strength than she expected from an injured man in a hospital bed. "You are the most beautiful woman I've ever known. And I don't only mean your stunning good looks. I saw through the chill that kept most people at bay. And I want to get to know you more." He blinked and ran his long fingers down the side of her face. "Much more."

Alexis gazed down at this man, who somehow saw the real version of her from the start. Maybe, just maybe, they could figure out some kind of a future together, even with so many moving parts. But she didn't have to do this alone anymore. *God, you see me and know me and love me...*

"Alexis? Are you trying to work out all the details and plan all the things to perfection when we only need to go one step at a time?"

Caught. She wrinkled her nose.

He shook his head. "I can read you like a book."

The verses she read from Mr. Wiebe's Bible came to mind. "You're not the only one."

He kissed her hands. "Then let's take this slowly. Pray. Talk. Listen. What do you say? It *is* Christmas..."

"My goodness, don't remind me. And Carla and Rhys's wedding is in four days." For the first time in months, wedding plans hadn't consumed Alexis. She pulled back and perched on the edge of the bed. "Be my date?"

"Excuse me?"

"Be my date for the wedding. My plus one. I prided myself on not needing anyone, but I think I'm allowed to change my mind. Maid of honor's prerogative." She squared her shoulders.

"Well then, yes. I would love to be your date. And I think I could get used to being your plus one." He stifled a yawn. "Although right now, I think I need to get my beauty sleep."

"And I have a hundred-and-one things to do. I'll check in on you later." Alexis picked up her purse. "Oh, wait." She bent over and kissed him on the lips with a decent dose of pent-up passion that left him wide-eyed and grinning like a fool. "Now I only have one hundred things to do."

EPILOGUE

"That was truly the most amazing wedding I've ever attended." Tom's heart was ready to burst clean out of his rented tux. "Seriously, you pulled off an extravaganza today. What a gift for your sister and her new husband."

Alexis threaded her arm through his as they strolled to the back of Carla and Rhys's cabin. Twinkling lights and snowflakes decorated every branch, and swept paths allowed guests to wander around the property as the celebrations wound down.

"Thank you. For the compliment but for being here, too." She rested her head against his good shoulder.

"I wouldn't have missed it. The bride and groom's ice dance? Magnificent. Nice work, coach."

"Thanks. They had fun, and all the guests were surprised." Alexis expelled a long, drawn-out sigh.

"Tired?" The woman must be exhausted. This week had been wild. Now, most of the guests had gone, leaving the catering crew to pack up the kitchen.

"You know I'll never admit to being tired." Alexis

pulled him toward the empty seating area on the back deck. "But let's sit. For your sake, of course."

"Of course. Although I've literally been sitting the whole time."

"You're recuperating."

"I'm fine. Painkillers are doing their thing." Tom sat next to her on the rattan loveseat. "Are you chilly?"

Alexis nestled deeper into the fur cape resting on her shoulders and slipped her hand into his. "Content. I'm so happy for Carla and Rhys. It's been a rough journey for them, but I see now how much they love one another and how much they've both grown."

Tom squeezed her fingers. "They're not the only ones who have grown, you know."

"Oh, I know. This past week has been a journey."

"For us both."

"For us all." She waved her other hand around the back of the property. "The newlyweds have exciting plans for this place, and I'm so happy they're going to be close by. I didn't realize how much I'd missed Carla until she came back into my life."

Tom enjoyed watching the sisters together. And he'd even met their parents, who flew in for the wedding from their missionary work in India. They were a fascinating family. One he would be privileged to know better. He smoothed his fingers over his trim beard. All he had left in England was his beloved Granny. Now, he had a grandfather here in Hollybrook. How was he going to navigate all this?

Tom lifted Alexis's hand to his lips and kissed each finger. "I wish I could be close by."

"Me, too." She snuggled into his side. "I know I have my Happily Ever After bookstore to manage—but is it wrong to long for my fairy tale ending in my personal life? I've always resisted the notion of finding my very own prince and settling down. But now..."

"Are you calling me your prince?" Tom pulled back and faced her. "Because I rather like that. And I believe if God wants us to be together, we'll find a way."

"He'll find a way." A genuine smile lit up her face. "And in the meantime, when I look into the emerald eyes of old Mr. Wiebe, I'll see a little piece of you."

His heart squeezed. "I'm going to miss you, beautiful. But I intend to make the most of the next three weeks while I'm here."

Alexis blinked back tears. "Hey, we can't be sad. It's Christmas Eve. Are you ready to open one gift tonight?"

"So ready." He chuckled. No need to think of goodbyes yet.

Alexis stood and walked over to the back door. She was stunning in her long, green velvet dress, which hugged her figure in all the right places. Her long blonde hair was curled into ringlets that cascaded down her back on top of the white fur cape. *Imagine what she would look like as a bride...*

"Okay, here we go." She shut the door and hurried back, carrying two wrapped gifts. "Merry Christmas, handsome." She handed him a rectangular present and perched on the loveseat, her blue eyes sparkling. "Open it up."

"Thank you." Tom tugged at the green ribbon and let it fall to his lap. "This is very book shaped." He wiggled his eyebrows.

"You're very bookish." She winked.

"Fair." He ripped open the shiny silver paper and pulled out a tan leather journal. Exquisite and soft to the touch. He ran his fingers over the engraved words on the front: Happily Ever After.

"You can start a new story now. Maybe our story? One with no more secrets." Her cheeks pinked. Was this coy, shy, slightly insecure Alexis? So many facets to this diamond of a woman.

"No more secrets. Thank you so much for this. I love it." He set the journal on the seat and took her face in his hands. "And I'm falling in love with you, Alexis James. Just so we're clear on that." He kissed her gently on the lips and nodded at the square box on her lap. "It's your turn."

❋

Alexis took a deep breath. Everything about this man, everything about this day, and everything about this place was magical. Yet, at the same time, so very real. She looked down and chuckled. "Do I recognize the wrapping style of a certain sister of mine?"

"I may have had a little assistance. I wanted it to be pretty." He pointed to his recovering shoulder. "Plus…"

"No need to explain. It's lovely." Alexis untied the familiar Happily Ever After red ribbon and tore away the gold wrapping paper to reveal a white cardboard box. "What have we here?" She lifted the lid and grinned. The top of a glass dome. "You bought me a snow globe?"

This man was wonderful in every way. He read her like a book from the beginning. He saw through the fictitious pages she had created for everyone else and honed in on her heart. He accepted her for who she was and helped her to find a way back to the God who loved her unconditionally. Gave her hope for a fairy tale ending like the one she dreamed of as a child with her very first snow globe.

With care, she lifted the orb from the box and studied the winter scene inside. A tiny man and woman bundled up wearing hats and scarves stood side-by-side in the snow—and both carried a stack of books. Alexis let out a cry of delight. "Where on earth did you find this? It's absolutely perfect."

"I had a few days recuperating and online shopping with my laptop this week. I wanted to replace the one that smashed outside the bookstore on our first encounter." He tilted his head. "You like it?"

"I love it." She shook the precious gift and the orb filled with tiny dancing snowflakes. "And in case you were wondering, I'm falling in love with you, Tom Harrington." She cupped the back of his head and pulled him in for a kiss that would warm them both to the tips of their toes.

"Wow." Tom blinked. "I guess you really like snow globes."

"I really like *you*. When I fall, I fall hard. So you know our story is going to be spectacular." Something caught her eye. "Hey, would you look at that?" Alexis stood and pulled Tom up next to her.

Clutching her snow globe, she led him to the edge of the back porch. They lifted their faces to the inky night sky and watched giant fluffy flakes dance and swirl and fall right alongside them.

Merry Christmas to me.

THE END

If you enjoyed this book, please consider leaving a review on your favorite retailer.

Want more books from Anaiah Press?
Join our Review Team!

And don't forget to sign up for the Anaiah Press Readers' Newsletter so you can stay up to date on all our new releases, our authors, and sales!

ABOUT THE AUTHOR

A published, award-winning Christian author, Laura writes heartwarming encouragement for your soul—especially in her numerous romantic suspense novels, as well as her teen fiction, marriage, and children's books. Laura is a hope*writers certified writing coach, a book-loving chocoholic mom and nanny, and is married to her high school sweetheart. Originally from the UK, they now live the empty nest life in Kelowna, British Columbia, with their French bulldog!

www.laurathomasauthor.com

ALSO BY LAURA THOMAS

Flight to Freedom Series:

The Glass Bottom Boat

The Lighthouse Baby

The Orphan Beach

The Christmas Cabin

Manufactured by Amazon.ca
Bolton, ON